Praise for *Into Bones L*

"*Into Bones Like Oil* is sinewy, disorientating, and devastat... g all the best ghost stories are."
PAUL TREMBLAY, author of *A Head Full of Ghosts* and
The Cabin at the End of the World

"Warren delivers a tale of creeping dread. Dora is in a house that we all know and despise from traveling, but where the guests are used as conduits. For Dora, the haunting by her past may be worse than anything supernatural and in Warren's hands, the horrific encroaches inexorably on the familiar. Recommended."
TADE THOMPSON, author of *Rosewater* and
The Murders of Molly Southbourne

"An amazingly talented voice out of Australia. You must read her work."
ELLEN DATLOW

"This dark, ethereal novella by Warren ... will especially appeal to horror readers who appreciate melancholic and atmospheric stories."
PUBLISHERS WEEKLY

"Beautifully written and profoundly disturbing, an evocative meditation on sorrow and loss, a ghost story in which the most terrifying specters come from within."
TIM WAGGONER, author of *The Forever House*

"Dark, disturbing, visceral."
LINDA HEPWORTH, NB MAGAZINE (5 STARS)

"Warren stirs awake an everyday fear that comes at you one hundred and one ways ... an accomplished story that is most unsettling."
EUGEN BACON, AUREALIS MAGAZINE

"A gripping and idiosyncratic story of horror and redemption ... the uncanny is actually the normality, and what we call 'normality' is actually the real horror."
SEB DOUBINSKY, author of the City-States Cycle series

ALSO BY KAARON WARREN

NOVELS

Slights
Walking the Tree
Mistification
The Grief Hole
Tide of Stone

COLLECTIONS

The Grinding House
The Glass Woman
Dead Sea Fruit
Through Splintered Walls
Cemetery Dance Select: Kaaron Warren
The Gate Theory
Exploring Dark Short Fiction #2: A Primer to Kaaron Warren

into
bones
like
oil

kaaron warren

Meerkat Press
Atlanta

ISBN-13 978-1-946154-42-2 (Paperback)
ISBN-13 978-1-946154-43-9 (eBook)

Library of Congress Control Number: 2019948180

This is a work of fiction. Names, characters, businesses, places, events and incidents are either the products of the author's imagination or used in a fictitious manner. Any resemblance to actual persons, living or dead, or actual events is purely coincidental.

Cover art by S.A. Hadi Hasan

Printed in the United States of America

Published in the United States of America by
Meerkat Press, LLC, Atlanta, Georgia
www.meerkatpress.com

For my Green Shed girls, for providing me with so much inspiration, support and friendship.

FIRST DAY
TUESDAY
NIGHT

The reception desk sat empty when Dora arrived at nine p.m. Good. That was the plan. The key to her room was in a lock box that wasn't locked ("It looks locked, that's the main thing," the landlord had told her). The key was there, along with a grease-stained sheet of rules and conditions (*No Cooking In The Rooms*) and a hand-drawn map showing her where to find her bedroom.

She was on the ground floor, although it was really the lower ground level now since the building had sunk further into the ground over the years. She passed the doorway her map indicated opened into the breakfast room (*7 a.m.–8 a.m. sharp*). The room was dark except for the light of the hallway spilling in, but she could see six or seven tables already set up. Each table was laid for one person and she smiled; that was one less thing to worry about. The idea of having to eat with a stranger horrified her. She could barely stand eating with her own family. She thought she could smell bacon, but there was also mustiness and something else, like hot metal.

Someone had hand lettered a sign for the bathroom door— *vacant*—and that was a relief too, unless someone thought it was funny to turn the sign over when someone else was inside. She glanced up and down the hallway and, seeing no one, ducked into the bathroom, flipping the sign. The other side said: *fuck off I'm in here*.

The bathroom's floor and walls were tiled in pale purple streaked with gold. It gave the room an odd glow because the pale green glass-globed light fixture was set high in the ceiling and dimmed by dust and dead insects. The toilet was old but clean. There was no sign of spare toilet paper in the room. Against the wall was a shower and bath combination with a large, pale purple bathtub that sported rust stains and paint chips. The shower curtain was moldy and stained, but at least it existed. She hated showering without one.

She'd wash later, once she figured out who was around and where they were.

She listened at the bathroom door and, hearing nothing, stepped into the hallway. She flipped the sign back to *vacant*. There were three doors off this stretch, one marked *linen*, with a lock, the others numbered. It was very quiet, but from each room came a slow murmur, a hum like a one-sided conversation.

She heard the gentle ticking of a large clock but couldn't see one.

The map said her room lay at the end of the hall. The key was small and flimsy, and she hoped it would work. She was relieved when it turned smoothly as it must have done a thousand times before.

Dora slid the door open. It was lightweight, shaking in the track as it moved. It would provide very little security. But then she was in an inner-city rooming house, so her expectation of security was low.

Her room had once been the foyer, when the house was much smaller and the entrance faced the other way. Now, after renovations and changes, it faced an alleyway. The old front door, now most of one of the walls, was covered with clothes hooks of many kinds. Her wardrobe. She thought previous tenants must have hammered the hooks in as there was nowhere else to hang clothes. There was no chest of drawers in the room, only one shelf over the bed, set into the wall. It looked like the place where, decades ago when a family lived here and milk was delivered to the door, the milkman would have put the bottles. She didn't remember those days, but her grandmother did, once wistfully and now as if it were still the case, as if milk was delivered each morning. There were six or seven books on the shelf.

Dora had very little with her. One small suitcase that she'd used as a seat and a pillow over the last week. There was no room to lay her suitcase out on the floor so she hefted it onto the bed. Opening the zip, she threw back the lid. She hung T-shirts and skirts and pants, two of each, on the hooks, folded her underwear onto the shelf. She had one book (*Chicken Soup for the Grieving Soul*) but no photos. She zipped the suitcase closed, lifted it off the bed, and placed it upright on the floor. Once she covered it with a pillowcase or a towel it would be a fine bedside table.

She moved the seven books, all by R.L. Stephenson (*Confessions of the Dead, Parts I–V, Lore of the Sea,* and *The Wreck*) from the shelf and placed them beside her suitcase. There was a blue bottle she left on the shelf, and—beside it—she placed two children's hairbrushes, pink and run through with strands of hair.

It was dead quiet outside. She hadn't eaten since lunch but was loath to go out. She wished she could leave by the old front door, but it was nailed shut. At least she had a window, a bay window looking onto the alleyway. Thick lace curtains covered it, and successive tenants had layered paper over the window for privacy, but someone had scratched a small square at the top to let light in.

She placed her book on the suitcase-table. She had half a cheese sandwich she'd saved from lunch so she ate that, then turned the light out and changed. The single bed creaked as she climbed into it, and the sheets felt slightly clammy. The rooming house shifted and she could hear footsteps, voices, cars outside. She could hear the ticking of the old clock. She heard something heavy being dragged, and a creaking noise where the door used to be, as if that door was being opened.

She sat up. The door was only a reach away, and she could see by the streetlight leaking through the layers on the window and streaming through the bare patch. She could feel when she touched it that the door was nailed shut.

She lay back down, hoping for sleep.

It had been many months since she'd slept well. Even before the children disappeared and were found, her worries had weighed her down, kept her awake and thinking when all she wanted was blessed sleep.

Even when her mother looked after the children and she was on her own, still she couldn't sleep. Back then, she'd convinced herself her ex-husband was a monster, and she sat curled up in an armchair (one they'd paid a fortune for, which she'd never regretted) swamped by the large blanket crocheted by her grandmother, holding her phone, waiting for the call to confirm he'd taken them, that her children were kidnapped by their own father, the man who'd loved her once.

The call never came. The children were always fine at her mother's.

Dora pulled the blanket up under her chin. It felt clammy and smelled faintly of wet hair and bleach.

A gentle noise streamed from a corner of the room: the rhythmic wash of the sea rolling into shore and back. The sound came from a speaker in the ceiling. She'd heard about this, the white or pink noise that would supposedly help her sleep. Over that, she could hear the upstairs neighbor moving around. It sounded like they were dragging furniture and bouncing a ball and throwing glasses onto the floor—all at the same time.

She was tired. Very, very tired at her core. The body shuts down, sleeps when sick or starving or dying. You only had to look at footage of starving children to see that.

SECOND DAY
WEDNESDAY
BREAKFAST

She slept fitfully, must have slept because she dreamed of people in the room, walking over her bed, standing over her, watching. At the time she'd thought they were real and froze in her bed, unwilling to move, thinking they were the other tenants. They'd rifle her shelf, her pockets, find nothing, leave. If she kept still they might not realize she was there.

It wasn't real, though. No one was there.

On awakening (so, again, she must have slept), she forgot where she was for a moment. How small the space was. At first she thought she'd been buried alive.

The house sat quiet at six a.m. She gathered her things, the bare minimum of toiletries: a toothbrush, toothpaste, hairbrush, shampoo, soap. She'd had a whole bathroom of crap at home, shelves of it, and there was a certain pleasure in now having so little.

Her towel was thin but good quality once. Left behind by a tenant, perhaps.

She slid open her door and peeked out. The hallway was as empty as it had been the night before, so she stepped out, slid her door closed, and locked it. Everything looked different in the morning light. Outside her door she saw there was a small bookcase containing *Confessions of the Dead, Parts VI–X* and some historical romances. She wondered if everyone had a similar collection: science fiction books in one, the next full of crime novels. She wondered if anyone had ever touched these books beyond the apparent librarian who had placed them.

There were paintings on the walls, all of them dark depictions of sea wrecks from various eras. The floor was linoleum, although she could see remnants of old carpet in some of the corners, an indication of lazy renovations in the past, or perhaps a lack of funds to complete the job.

She could hear the clang of dishes in the breakfast room; staff preparing for the onslaught, perhaps.

She showered quickly. There was no lock on the door. (How could there be no lock on the door?) She moved the old wooden chair up against it, so that at least the door would open slowly if it was pushed. The water didn't heat beyond lukewarm and the pressure was weak, but it felt good to wash her hair, her face, and to dress in the fresh shirt, underwear, and pants she'd saved for when she was clean herself.

~

The first thing she noticed in the breakfast room was the wall color. It was a sickly yellow and she wondered about it: why? Was it once white and had slowly stained to this? It made her feel faintly ill, but the smell of bacon, of coffee, of toast made her stomach grumble and she knew she would happily eat two plates of food if she could.

There were three men in the breakfast room. One standing near the window, looking out. One sat at a table eating his breakfast. One fussing behind the food service area, a tea towel over his arm. He was in his sixties, receding gray hair, greasy comb-over, acne-scared face.

"I'm Roy," he said, "And you've made it to breakfast. Well done!"

She wasn't sure how to respond, although it did feel like an achievement to have made it through the door.

"You must have come in late last night. How'd you sleep? My office is behind reception if you ever need me for anything. Anything at all."

He smiled at her. His teeth were crooked, discolored, but when he closed his mouth and smiled he looked almost handsome. "I'm the landlord. Boss of all I survey. And writer. A ghost writer, you might say. R. L. Stephenson, in the flesh." He didn't shake her hand, which she was grateful for.

"Congratulations," she said, unsure what you were supposed to say to a writer.

"I'm Larry," the second man said. He stood up from his meal

and held out his hand. He was enormous, easily six-foot-eight with broad shoulders, a strong jaw. He was in his sixties, too, but looked far healthier than Roy. She shook his hand and felt pain all the way up to her shoulder; he was so strong even this gentle gesture hurt. Her hand was swamped by his. He shook her hand six times; she could see him counting.

"I hate odd numbers," he said. He must have been a powerful man when he was younger. His hair was white now, tufts of it on his chest. He wore a blue singlet and an unbuttoned checked shirt.

"Help yourself," Roy said. "It's boiled eggs and bacon and toast today. Good to get in early before the hordes arrive." He was neat, with his hair slicked back. She would have said Brylcream, like her grandfather used. He spoke carefully and clearly, like a drunk pretending not to be. He waved his arm at a blackboard notice:

Monday spaghetti on toast
Tuesday baked beans on toast
Wednesday Boiled eggs on toast with bacon
Thursday Cereal diet day
Friday Herrings
Saturday sausages and toast
Sunday eggs and bacon and pastries

Dora piled her plate with hot food. There were no pastries or yogurt, no fresh fruit, but she hadn't expected that. The coffee was the good sort of instant and she almost wept at the sight of it. She ate quickly, hoping to be gone before any of the other tenants spoke to her.

The ticking of the clock was louder in the breakfast room. She saw it sitting on the mantel. What a magnificent piece it was: a large, dark-wood mantle clock, curved along the top and straight down the sides. The clock face was ornate, with a rounded, yellowed, glass face, copper hands. The second hand ticked smoothly but not noticeably; mesmerizing. There was a red segment at three minutes before twelve and one at three minutes before six. She hadn't seen this before and stood close to it, wondering what it meant.

"It's called the three minutes of silence." This was the third man in the room, standing now beside her. He was remarkable among the rest of them. Strong and healthy looking. Handsome. "For distress signals to come through. So they'd maintain radio silence at those times."

He smelled clean and fresh and Dora was glad she'd showered before breakfast. He was wearing slacks and a shirt but no tie.

"Luke," he said, holding out his hand. "Ex-navy, but it's in the blood, as they say."

"Dora," she said. "Ex-wife," and she felt her cheeks burn with the stupidity of the statement.

"Good to know," he said and he winked at her. "I'll catch you tonight. Gotta go out and bring in the bacon."

Dora felt uncomfortable following him out of the room so she sat at her table with another cup of coffee. She'd wait three minutes, she thought.

The room was quiet until a woman rushed in at a few minutes to eight. She was barefoot, wearing layers of soft pastel clothing, including a diaphanous skirt, a vest, scarves, and a belt hung with bells.

"You just made it, Freesia! How'd you sleep?" Roy said.

"Like a fucken baby," she said. She sat at the next table to Dora and ate, watching her. Dora felt uncomfortable and quickly drank the last of her coffee, wanting to leave.

"You an addict?" Freesia said to her. Dora noticed the woman didn't say, "have you ever been," because once an addict, always an addict. She shook her head. "This is what it feels like. It gets in your blood, buries itself into your brain. It's like a tiny man in your head pulling the levers."

"Okay," Dora said.

"I haven't slept in years. It's the things I've seen. No one should see what I've seen."

Dora didn't really want to know what this woman had seen. Her head was already full of images she couldn't forget. Her daughters, looking so serene, undamaged. But on the inside? Where she couldn't see, could only imagine? On the inside. The dishes on the kitchen bench from breakfast that morning, whole poached eggs congealing, toast with a single bite taken. The coroner's report stated her girls had empty stomachs, but she had relented, driven through McDonald's for Egg McMuffins and considered herself a saint for not saying,

How do you eat that and not what's at home, but at the same time glad because their last words to her were "Thanks, Mum."

"So, how'd you find us, Dora?" Freesia said. "We've all got sleep issues here. People who can't sleep are like backpackers and homeless people, they share information about good places to stay. Someone told you about this place, right? It's word of mouth."

"My sister-in-law suggested it. Don't know where she heard about it."

"Does she hate you?" Freesia said. "She must hate you."

Dora thought about her sister-in-law's face, so filled with disgust her eyes were almost gone. "No, she loves me," Dora said.

"Well, you're welcome no matter what," Roy said. "You've got the best room in the house." Freesia laughed, as did Larry. Roy joined in. "When someone shifts out or dies you can have their room, I promise."

"Who was in my room before me?"

"Why do you ask?"

"I feel like they are still there. Someone in my room I didn't invite."

"We don't think about that. There's only now, who's there now. Otherwise we're all living in the shadow of others.

The smell of breakfast followed her back to her room.

SECOND DAY
WEDNESDAY
NIGHT

In the late afternoon, once she'd listened at the door to make sure the hallway was clear, Dora left to go to the shops. She needed some basic things: packaged food for dinner, or tins, although she was tired of tuna and it made her think of her youngest daughter, how she'd cried about eating the lovely big tuna fish and how they'd all laughed at her.

She saw the sign on Roy's closed door—*private staff only*—in the same lettering as all the other signs. She heard movement behind the door and walked quickly to get out without being seen, but it was too late.

"Ah!" he said. "Going for a walk?"

"Just getting a bit of shopping."

"Excellent idea. I might join you if you don't mind. Give us a chance to get to know each other."

His hair had lost its neatness and hung in his eyes. He was dressed in baggy tracksuit pants and a loose T-shirt that once had a logo but now was faded beyond legibility.

"So, you first or me?" he said as they walked. She shook her head, mortified. She wouldn't speak about her life, not to this man or to any other.

"Me, then. Now, the thing you have to know about me is that I am a great believer in fate."

He told her he was the grandson of a woman who was cut from her hanged mother's stomach. No sign of the father, probably a prison guard. Nobody took responsibility. Nobody owned up. That baby was only saved because there was a midwife watching the execution and she noticed the dead woman's stomach moving. "Cut her open!" she called, and the baby was set free, born screaming like the demons were taking her.

Kept in care by nuns, she was always a very cautious girl. She never broke the law. She became a nurse herself and kept herself to herself until the butcher asked her to marry him and she did. He was a handsome man, ruddy-faced and fit. She was strong and healthy; she'd never taken a drink, not a single time.

Their child was Roy's father, who grew to be a very handsome young man. He became an actor and a model. He had six children by six different mothers. Roy was the last of them, born when his father was over fifty and ready to settle at last, but too late, a heart attack took him before Roy's third birthday.

"I am a great believer in fate. Fate had that nurse at my great-grand-mother's hanging. Fate kept my father alive long enough to help make me, and fate has kept me alive. I've always known I had to do something with my life."

"So you're running a rooming house?"

"You know it's more than a rooming house. You wouldn't have come, otherwise. You need help to sleep. Everyone does who comes to me. You will sleep well here at The Angelsea. No doubt about that at all. It's my little contribution."

In the small local supermarket Roy bought cigarettes and the newspaper. Dora bought cheese crackers, bananas, beef jerky. Her oldest daughter hated bananas, even the smell of them, so they'd never had them in the house.

"I might go for a walk around the block," she said. "I'll see you back at the house."

If he insists on coming with me I'm moving out, she thought, but luckily he didn't.

~

There was no sign of Roy as she approached The Angelsea on her return. It was a hard walk up the hill and she had to pause a few times. But she liked the feel of her muscles, liked the sense of actually working at something, if only for a little while. She hadn't been able to see the building well the night before, but now she saw it was four storeys tall, made of dark red brick, marked with decades of pollution. There were many small windows. The walls were covered with ivy and there was moss in the mortar. A veranda graced the front, the floorboards damaged by the sun, almost burned in places. The railings were recently replaced; someone wanting to keep it safe, so that no one could fall or tip over the edge.

The front door was quite small. It used to be the servants' entrance, decades ago. But so many rooms had been added and other houses built around The Angelsea, the original front door and foyer—Dora's room—were blocked off. Rickety stairs clung to the side of the house, in dark shadows.

Taller buildings surrounded the house now, blocking most of the light.

The sun was beautifully warm and she sat on the front step, closing her eyes and letting it wash over her.

Luke appeared behind her, like a ghost.

He said, "Bloody lovely isn't it? That sun. Makes you forget for a minute, doesn't it?"

She didn't ask him *forget what*? He really was almost handsome.

But his eyes were ringed with shadow and his face gaunt. Those eyes were green, and his hairline was good. He was tidy and clean, with a neatly-ironed, well-fitted shirt. His haircut was military. She could see his scalp. He wore tight black jeans.

"Home from work already?"

"Yeah, I'm on a disability so I work short days. Blinding headaches. Nothing like coming home to The Angelsea to make a headache disappear." He winked at her; she'd have to get used to that.

"Shouldn't it be 'Anglesea'? I've been wondering about that."

"Yeah, poor bastard can't spell. Apparently there was a famous shipwreck at Anglesea so he named the place after that." Dora noticed the name was painted on a piece of driftwood she imagined must have come from the wreck. "Got it wrong. He shoulda just named it after our own shipwreck. Most of the town call it Shipwreck House, anyway."

They both turned to look down the hill. Dora could see some piles of metal on the rocks and on the sand down there. The beach was almost inaccessible, even by water.

The Barlington had struck ground there, all lives lost. At the time there were no communities in the area, so the shipwreck went unnoticed for weeks. Some may have survived the accident but couldn't find a way off the beach. It was the smell, they said, that led to the eventual discovery. Plus the clothing rolling into the beaches along the coast.

"Half the house is decorated with stuff he's pinched from down there. Pays the local kids to risk their lives getting it. Like those." He pointed at four large broken lights, anchored to the wall near the door.

Dora realized she needed to respond to him, so said, "Are these old ship danger lights or something?" She hated herself for the "or something." Her therapist had told her she needed to regain herself by standing by her own statements, but she couldn't help it.

"Yes! Fat lot of good they did. He pinched them from the crash site. He calls it beachcombing. Other people might call it looting. He used to have them set up to flash until one poor bloke killed himself over them."

"Like a fit or something?"

"Nah, he was a train driver, caused an accident, killed a heap of passengers. Apparently he reckoned the lights flashed wrong, but no one believed him. Gets the sack, wife leaves him, he comes to live here. Takes a room on the fourth floor, with a window looking down onto the water. It's my room, now. Of course Roy has to set those ship lights going so that every night the poor bastard up there watched them flashing on and off, on and off like train lights. Hung hisself. Up in my room. I dunno if you believe in ghosts or not, but sometimes I reckon he's there. Only he knows if it really was his fault. Who knows. Maybe it was deliberate. Maybe he just wanted to see what would happen. We're all a bit that way, aren't we? We're all so bored we'll try anything."

"Speak for yourself!" she said.

"You can come have a look if you want." He looked at her expectantly.

"I guess I could take a look," she said. She shuddered. The air was growing colder. She stood up and they went inside. The ticking of the clock seemed louder.

"Maybe someone's having an afternoon nap," Luke said, and she wished she was confident enough to ask him what he meant by that. A nap sounded good, though. Sometimes a nap worked.

Four flights of stairs to his room. The stairwell was dark and smelly, as if someone had used the ground floor for a toilet and the smell rose all the way up. The lino was old and slippery, so she clung on the handrail, when it was there. She grabbed Luke's shirt, and he took her hand. His was warm and dry.

"This is me," he said, pushing the stairwell door open. The sign said *fort floor*. "Nice and quiet up here. Just the woman next door."

She didn't know who he was talking about but had no more questions.

His door was solid, old, scratched with names and dates. He pushed it open.

Inside it was bright. He had a lot of windows, none of them with coverings. "Nice during the day, a pain at night," he said. "And you can't open any of the windows. Roy thinks it'll stop suicides, but it doesn't."

She could see now, as the sun fell, that artificial light poured in, even though they were four storeys up. Strong street lights and the security lights of the garment factory two doors down.

"Wow," she said. The room was obsessively neat, with all the books color-coded, glasses lined up on a small table, nothing left on the floor that shouldn't be there. It was four times the size of her room, but still small. No bathroom, no kitchen. Navy memorabilia filled the walls and made up most of the furniture; trunks, khaki rugs, anchors, plaques, knives, and what looked with a tiny replica landmine.

"If the ghost isn't here, he might be marching up and down the coast hill. You can see the track they've worn. See?"

Looking down, there was a path in the long grass.

"They?"

"Roy. And tourists sometimes." She could see other debris too: wood, metal, piles of each. He stood closer to her. "Near midnight, other times too, you can see ghosts walking up from the wreck. Over and over, trekking up and down. Roy reckons they need to speak their last words, but no one can hear them. I think they're just . . . lost." He was very close to her now. She stepped away to really look at him. His knuckles were unmarked, no scars, which was a good sign.

"Can you see them?"

"Not down there. But they come visit, up here at the house. Roy's pinched so much of their stuff they think this is where they belong."

His room smelled of Febreze. It was chemical, fake, but a nice change from mold, smoke, frying onions, sewage.

"It's moments like these I don't hate Shitwreck House," he said. She laughed.

"Would you like a drink?" he said. He lifted two nice glasses from a tiny covered table. Each had an anchor etched in gold. "I've got some vodka left over from something. Pinched it from my parents. They're pissheads who always forget what they've got."

"I'd love to meet them," she said. "You can tell them I'm your fiancée, and they'll pull out the champagne." Being with him, with anyone, was almost painful. But there were moments of pleasure in company. When the other person momentarily made her forget. So she smiled and put on the face that said, "I am an ordinary person capable of talking to you."

"We don't even know if we like each other yet," he said, handing her a glass full of vodka, no mixer. The glass had the word *Oceania* etched above the anchor. "Roy collected them," he said. "He reckons from the wreck, but I reckon from the op shop."

"What's a man like you doing in a place like this?" she said, instantly regretting it. No past, no future, just the present. In her real self, her real life, she wouldn't even contemplate sleeping with him. But here, time was contracted. Relationships would form and fall apart quickly.

Here, she was who he thought she was. Not who she really was.

And she knew she'd sleep with one of them. A couple of them, probably. Sex gave her a momentary feeling of being appreciated. Regardless of what happened before and after, you were loved in that moment. Even by someone who despised you.

She drank that glass and another, and then felt so good she stepped up to him and kissed him gently on the lips. He put his hands on her shoulder.

"Are you sure? I always like them to be sure." It wasn't until later she wondered who "they" were and how many there had been.

She nodded. He kissed her, holding her enclosed in his arms, then his hands moved down and cupped her arse. He had big hands. They felt so different from her ex-husband's. He had small hands, long fingers, he didn't have a gentle touch.

This man had a gentle touch.

From below, someone thumped. She could hear a muffled "shut the fuck up" and she blushed at the idea whoever it was could hear what they were doing.

"Don't mind her. Fucking lunatic. Fucking monster. If she's gonna whine, I reckon I'll wear my army boots. In fact, I might as well wear them."

He pulled a pair of boots on and stood, naked, before her.

Dora laughed till she wept as he danced for her.

Then they made love again.

He fell asleep straight after. She watched him, almost angry with envy at his peaceful face. She wondered what it would be like to sleep like that. She didn't want to mistrust a man again so soon.

She pulled her clothes on and went to the toilet. It was nicer than the one on her floor. Smaller, but then there were only three rooms to service. It felt warmer, too, maybe because the heat rose through the house. There was spare toilet paper on a stick by the bath.

His door had snicked shut. She knocked quietly but didn't want to waken him, so headed downstairs. Once near her bedroom she realized there was no way she'd sleep. She felt wired, wide awake, excited. She went down to look at the site of the wreck, following the path worn by looters, tourists, and, according to Luke, ghosts. The streetlights provided more than enough illumination for her to find her way.

It took longer than she thought and once she reached the edge of the cliff, she lost the energy to walk all the way down. She could see that the metal was very rusty, the wood mossy and cracked. Dora wondered that what was left of the vessel was still there. It was pulled up high on the beach where the tide couldn't reach it. Perhaps this—along with the containers, jars, and remnants of many other things she could see—was the real rubbish, all the good stuff long since taken.

She heard someone coming and hid behind one of the large bushes that lined the path. She didn't want to talk to anyone. She felt dirty and tired and not up to speech.

It was Roy. He held a large hook and seemed to be dragging something, but she couldn't see what. Behind him she thought she saw a line of bedraggled people. As they passed her she felt overwhelming sadness. Helplessness. Once they were gone she headed back to the rooming house, but the smell of fried food drew her to an all-night taxi drivers café, thankfully almost empty. She bought herself half-a-dozen dim sims to take back to her room.

Once there, she heard the clock ticking loudly and found herself chewing in time.

She checked her phone, but no one had called. She closed her eyes and tried to sleep, but the upstairs neighbor sounded like he was dancing in army boots.

The thought of it made her smile.

THIRD DAY
THURSDAY
BREAKFAST

Dora felt a physical reluctance to wake up, as if she was burrowed deep in a safe hole and someone had a rope tied around her ankle and was forcibly dragging her up to the surface. She'd slept, at least; she remembered dreams of ghosts with their fingers bitten off by thieves stealing their rings. And she had short nightmares of home, *her daughters sitting at the bench eating breakfast,* that she managed to rouse herself from. She was up early enough to shower before breakfast and did so, although she was made to feel uncomfortable by water already on the shower floor, and the faint scent of someone else's toilet visit. She didn't wash her hair because her towel was still damp, but she dressed in clean clothes and felt quite bright.

In the breakfast room, the clock ticked gently in the silence.

Dora sat in her corner breakfast spot. She knew she could skip the ordeal, eat muesli bars in her room, but there was something compelling about watching the daily parade.

Freesia came in before the others. Dora thought perhaps she'd been out all night.

"How'd you sleep?" Freesia asked her. "Everyone has a good night's sleep here. It's like being on board a ship, you know, rocking rocking rocking and you can hear the waves if you listen closely." She picked up untoasted bread, tore off the crusts and ate them, then balled the center into a sphere and popped that into her mouth like a pill.

"I think it's the sound coming through the speakers," Dora said. It was like the sea gently lapping at the shore. White noise? Pink noise? She wasn't sure which. "I slept well, but I felt like people were watching me."

"They were," Freesia whispered, then laughed, a high screech that set Dora's nerves on end. "I think of myself as a free spirit. Get it? Free Spirit . . . Free-Sia."

Dora thought that all this meant was she'd never finished school, had never held a job, certainly not one you had to apply for. Maybe fruit picking? A job where you just had to show up. She might be able to manage that.

"What's your born name?" Larry asked her. He and Roy had entered and headed directly to the food.

"Nah," Freesia said.

"Go on. What? Beryl? Fucken Ethel?"

"Ruth," she said finally, to shut him up.

"Jeeze," Roy said. "You lot should spend less time making fun of someone's name and more time figuring out how we'll get the coin for a bottle of booze."

"We could get a bottle of crap red," Freesia said. "I heard this trick that if you tip a bit of OJ into it, it tastes like good shit, not shit shit."

A new woman entered the room. Dora had heard shuffling in the night-time, and heavy breathing, but no arrival.

This woman was in her twenties. She was morbidly obese, dressed in clothing too big for her. It looked like she was wearing a bed sheet. Her hair was wet and her face shiny. Fresh from the shower, perhaps? Was she in there before Dora? But she didn't look refreshed.

Roy looked up from arranging cereal boxes. "Julia is awake! You look marvelous," he said. He'd combed his hair and was wearing a suit, looked almost ordinary.

Julia lifted her arms and twirled herself around. She had fold after fold of skin. She said, "Do I look skinnier? Come on, you bastard. I haven't eaten for a week. I must be skinnier."

"Breakfast?" Roy said. "Grapefruit followed by a shit ton of bacon?"

Quiet laughter around the room. "It's cereal day, Roy," Larry said. "Don't be a mongrel."

Julia sat down next to another new addition, a silver-haired man at the other corner table.

"Seriously, Dr. Adams," Julia said to him. "I was asleep for a week?"

"How do you feel?" the doctor said. He stood and washed his hands at the nearby basin.

"My throat is really sore. And I'm starving."

"Did you sleep well?"

"I don't know. I guess? But I don't feel like I was asleep for that long."

"This method has that effect in a way. It replicates the sense of coma, liked we talked about. Like your brother."

"Yeah but. He was in that coma for seven years."

"You can't sleep that long. Maybe one day we'll be able to replicate it," the doctor said.

"A whole week not having to think," she said. "It was beautiful. Like my brother said. You live your dream life. That's hard to wake up from." She stood up again and stretched. The mantelpiece clock ticked into the silence. "He went to sleep again," she said. "He hated being awake. Cried all the time. He felt so far behind all his friends. He had nothing, not even a high school diploma. He said he thought he had it sorted, but he woke up and he'd done nothing. Not that I've done a lot. But I got my beauty diploma."

"I got my hairdressing one!" Dora said. "I actually got a few awards for haircutting even."

"We should open a shop! Anyway. I missed him. Miss him. I'm eating enough for the two of us." She chuckled here, wanting Dora to laugh along, laugh at the fat girl joking about herself, but Dora didn't.

"I wish I could sleep," Dora said. "Forget for a while."

"They can help you."

The alarm went off at eight a.m., signaling the end of breakfast.

"Session's over," someone said.

Dora would learn that someone said that every day, and even those who hadn't been through therapy understood what it meant.

~

Dora washed her underwear and T-shirts in the shower, then took them into the small backyard hoping to dry them in the sun. Roy was there (he seemed to be everywhere), sitting on a milk crate, smoking a hand-rolled cigarette. On the washing line was money. A dozen or more damp notes.

Dora started hanging her clothes up. There were no clothespins, so she draped them over the lines.

"You probably need to wait here till they dry," Roy said. "People'll pinch anything."

Dora stood there, not knowing what to do.

"Pull up a pew," he said, indicating another milk crate. She couldn't think of anything worse, but sat without speaking. "Your upstairs neighbor is no longer with us. Should be quieter now," he said. "Until I go hunting for a new tenant."

"Okay," she said.

He said, "Every time some mongrel moves out I have to replace the fittings. These bastards even took the mirror. They're all cunts. You'll find out."

"I don't have a mirror in my room so don't think I pinched it when I leave." She was always careful to stay within the law.

"Nah, yours got pinched already. We might find one for you down at the wreck site."

"Isn't that called looting?" she said.

They both looked at the money, drying on the line.

"You'd be amazed what people leave behind here. Under the mattresses, mostly. I'm just doing a bit of money laundering."

Dora knew she was supposed to laugh, but the best she could manage was a smile. "So what happened to my neighbor? I thought they were quieter last night."

"Offed themselves. But some of these people are already dead before they're dead, if you know what I mean."

"Who cleans that up? You?"

"Muggins, as they say. I do most of it around here. I do the breakfast, but Freesia helps sometimes. We do have a cleaner comes in every now and then. Washes the linen and other stuff. I used to do it myself but had complaints, didn't I, Freesia?

The door slammed, Freesia with her arms full of wet washing. "Jeez, Roy. Get this shit off the line."

She hung out her underwear, all of it sexy, see-though, very small.

"Look at this sexy bitch," Roy said. "Ay? Check her out. Hippy on the outside, hooker on the inside."

"Fuck off, Roy. If you don't take this shit off I'm pinching it and spending it. You're a fucken limp-dicked loser so fuck off."

Roy's shoulders slumped. He stood up and plucked the notes

off the line. "You can leave whenever you want to," he said. Freesia kissed him on the cheek.

"You know you love me," she said. They watched Roy slink away, the notes shoved in his pockets.

"Come upstairs for a cuppa?" Freesia said to Dora. "I'm up the top there. It's like a crow's nest. Glass ceilings. Like sleeping under the stars."

"Maybe later," Dora said.

"You watch that Roy. I'm good at making him feel loved. It's my only talent, making men feel loved. You know? Respected. It doesn't work on men who are beloved or respected, only men like Roy."

Dora didn't know how Freesia managed it. Roy really was repulsive-looking, the smell of his cologne strong enough, evil enough, to singe nose hairs.

"He's an arsehole like all men. You watch it when he comes for the rent. He'll offer 'in kind' and he doesn't mean sex."

"What does he mean?"

"He'll want you to go to sleep for a day or two. And you'll talk. You'll talk non-stop, the voice of some shitty arsehole dead drowned sailor, and you'll wake up feeling like hell."

"I may not have the rent money."

"Then you might have to go to sleep for a day or two."

"That's . . . weird."

"Nobody lives here who wasn't born weird," Freesia said. "Haven't you noticed? This place is full of shipwreck stories. Most of us are fucken wrecks."

"Luke calls it Shitwreck House!"

"Yeah, well. Luke is a funny bastard, isn't he?" Freesia glared at her, lit a cigarette, and literally turned her back.

Dora decided she didn't mind if her things were stolen. She didn't want to stay there any longer. But then Freesia drifted off to sleep in the sun, the cigarette still between her fingers. Dora took it and stamped it out.

Freesia started to murmur.

In the sunshine there were shadows. Dora thought she could see the shape of a tall person, tall and thin, bending over, talking into Freesia's ear.

"Told him twice. Told him. Told him twice. Told him," Freesia said. Her voice was low and scratchy, rough.

Roy appeared in the yard. "What's she saying?"

"Listen yourself," Dora said. She couldn't bear to hear the voice anymore.

She headed back to her room, but the idea of sitting there in the dark on this sunny day made her feel pathetic, so she decided to go for a walk instead.

It was quiet. Along the corridor leading to the front entrance were old faded photographs in dented and marred mismatched frames. There were photos of a group of young cyclists, standing proudly beside their bikes. There were cups and tankards on shelves and china cats, dozens of them, all damaged in one way or another.

The mantelpiece clock ticked so loudly she could hear it halfway up the hallway and she wondered if anyone had serviced it in the last few decades.

Outside, she saw Roy up ahead, stumbling with purpose, and she followed him to the shipwreck site. He carried a hook over his shoulder.

Even in daylight the beach was hard to get to, although she could see the path Roy walked. There was a section of shoreline covered in clothing. Roy would tell her later that somehow this happened day by day, clothing would wash in and gather in piles. The day was warm but not hot. Still she could see a shimmering miasma over the beach, like the road on a summer's day.

In the daytime there was a clarity about the wreckage that laid out what had happened. Even now there were deep gouges in the ground, which was littered with metal and wood. Very little of value. Luke had told her Roy bought a lot of his stuff from a shipbreaking town in India: a satellite mast, porthole glass, lino, security doors, coffee machines, armchairs, crockery, fridges, anchors, ropes, cupboards, mirrors, tables, plates, jam jars, colanders, fire exit signs. The lights he had out the front of the building, which looked welcoming but did little to warn what was ahead. Roy said he dived for and found the treasures himself; Luke's version seemed more likely.

She watched as Roy headed back up the path. She saw images attached to him like limpets, shapes of people—a young boy, an older girl. He dragged another along with his hook, *a half-naked man,* she thought. And yet another he held out his hand to, and he walked along that way as if leading someone to a pleasant picnic spot.

Dora wasn't seeing what she was seeing, she knew that. She was hungry, hadn't eaten since breakfast and then it was only cereal. Her vision was blurred. He was just an ugly man, and those shapes she saw? The people she imagined? That was only the sea spray around him, his own rising heat, perhaps.

She walked home via the supermarket, stopping to pick up some more cheese crackers and a packet of lollies. She had a sweet tooth and couldn't eat lollies when the girls were around because they'd want one, or they'd steal one from the cupboard when she wasn't looking and she'd have to discipline them, which she hated doing.

She could see where her room was, on the corner of the house. From the outside it looked as if the door could open, but she knew it was nailed shut. The ground in front of the door was over-run with high grass.

When she reached her room she found a note under the door.

Am home from work. Come up and see me when you get home. I have vodka and chips. Luke.

She showered first. The floor and shower were dry this time, far more pleasant. While she showered she thought of things she could talk to Luke about. How easily she was pleased; how she wanted very little because she had very little and was everyone like that? And about the beach and what lay on it and Roy and his books and his rent and about what Freesia had said, about sleeping and ghosts.

She'd ask him all of that. It would mean they'd have something to talk about.

She checked her phone but no one had called.

She went out the back to get her washing and some of it was gone. Her own fault. No one to blame but herself.

~

Luke wore a nice blue shirt and ironed jeans. She felt old and ugly in her own clothes, wished she had work clothes like he had, something respectable that would make her look as if she was capable of holding down a job.

"How'd you sleep, gorgeous?" he said, and he kissed her gently on the side of the mouth. He smelled very faintly of sweat but also of aftershave, not like Roy's, like something that cost actual money.

"How was work?" she asked, because you did. She didn't know what he did for a living and he didn't tell her.

"Yeah, not bad. Better to be home, though."

"Yeah, it's the little things, isn't it?" she said, and she told him about her thoughts, about how the little things could make her happy.

"I don't get why you live here, though! You should be able to afford somewhere else."

"I like it here because there are needy women who ask for little," he said, straight-faced until tears pricked her eyes. "Kidding! It's just an interesting place to live. That's all."

"I went down to the beach today." This was the next topic she'd rehearsed. "It was so weird. There are all these clothes washed up. And metal bits and other things. From the shipwreck?"

"Most of that was pinched long ago. Not all of them died in the wreck, you know. Some were murdered on the beach fighting for treasure."

"What sort of treasure?"

"They thought there might be gold. You know, people's wedding rings, that kind of thing. Whatever there was, it's long gone."

He poured them a drink and opened a packet of chips. "Looters are arseholes. You know they swoop in after a natural disaster. Flood or fire or cyclone. Army has to step in half the time. Shipwreck stealing is bad enough but after disasters? They're pinching from a person's home or shop, you know? So when that person finally gets back, they've lost even more than they should have."

"Would you call Roy a looter?"

Luke said, "I guess he would say it's 'spoils of war.' No one else will look after you. You need to look out for yourself and your family."

This was the moment when ordinary people would ask about family—his and hers, who are they, where are they, what do your kids do, where did you meet your wife, your husband—but no. These two glanced at each other and neither asked the questions. Both understood family was not to be discussed. Many at the rooming house would be the same. Family is past; there is only the present.

"Anyway, there's a bit of a thing Saturday. Our version of a party. We're all going. They call it a Ship Wreck."

"Oh, I probably won't."

"You should come. Bring something. Booze is best. You can come with me."

"Freesia may not like that."

"Freesia . . . Freesia will fuck anything with a dick and then think she's married to it. One of those."

Then he tugged her on to the bed and made love to her. Tender man, tender and gentle and it made her cry to feel that way although she buried her face in the pillow so he couldn't see.

~

He fell asleep quickly again, with his solid arm across her. She needed the toilet but was anxious about going. She didn't want to leave this warm bed and go back to her hole in the wall. She didn't want to wake him. She didn't want to prop his door open in case someone came in.

In the end she had to get up and go. She'd go back to her own bed, curl up there in the damp sheets (why weren't his damp?) and try to sleep. She pushed open the bathroom door and stepped outside.

"There you are."

Dora jumped a meter in the air.

"Jeezus."

Roy stood there, beside the door, in the shadows.

"Freesia's falling asleep. Do you want to come and listen? You can hear for yourself what a pack of cunts they are."

"Listen to what?"

"The ghosts talk. I saw you on the cliff. You know what I dragged back. Come listen to them." He tried to take her hand but she resisted. "I feel like I can talk to you. You understand me."

They climbed the narrow stairs up to Freesia's room and met

Dr. Adams on his way down. The doctor squeezed past Dora, face towards her, pressing against her. He had an erection, she was sure.

"All sleepy?" Roy said, nodding at Julia.

"Nice and sleepy. She'll be out for a day," the doctor said. "You next," he whispered to Dora.

She and Roy continued up the stairs. "Only if you want it," Roy said. "It's good, though. People come out feeling brand new."

She knew that wasn't true. She'd seen Julia after her big sleep, spoken to her; the woman had been drained.

Freesia's room wasn't much larger than Dora's, but it was light and the ceiling higher. As Freesia had mentioned, the ceiling was made of glass. At first Dora thought it was brilliantly painted but saw that the stars, the deep dark sky, were the real thing.

"Gorgeous room," she whispered.

Roy nodded. "When she goes you can have it," he said. A sick part of Dora enjoyed this favoritism.

Freesia lay on top of the covers. She was wearing baby doll pajamas, pink and frilly. The panties were slightly shifted to one side and Dora readjusted them.

There was one chair in the room and Roy took that. "I need to take notes," he said. He laid a tape recorder on the bed and settled with a large notebook and pen. Dora knelt beside the bed as if she were praying.

It was silent for a while, then Freesia began to speak.

"Aw. Aw. That's mine, that's yours, that's mine. That's mine. That suit of clothing, that bolt of material. Mine."

"One of the looters," Roy whispered.

Dora shook her head. It was Freesia, talking in her sleep. But she could hear a *tick tick tick* in her ears, her blood beating, and she could smell a saltiness in the air, she was sure, and if she looked hard, tilted her head, he was there.

He was there.

Half-naked, his hair knotted with seaweed and rotted matter, he bent over Freesia and whispered to her. His fingers were half bitten off, half broken. Dora fell backwards, banged her head and thought: *not a nightmare. I'm awake.*

The ghost hadn't paused; didn't see her. For that she was grateful.

"Those sheets, those blankets, the barrels of apples. That beer. Oh, those suits of clothing. The napkin rings. The rings. I bit her finger off to get this one," and Dora could see him lift his hand. He looked at it quizzically, as if lost.

"That bolt of material," he said.

Then he vanished.

"He'll be back. As long as she's asleep, he'll be back. This is good stuff."

Dora's mouth was numb. She felt as if she were in another body, looking down.

"It's a bit scary the first time. But they're just like you and me. They all want their last words to be heard. Until those words are heard, they can't be free."

"This can't be."

"Oh, but it is. I've heard confessions. I've had 'tell her I love her.' I have clues to where money is buried because they don't want it to rot away, but it is long gone. One of these days I'll strike it big, though, just you watch."

"How are you not scared?"

"Oh, I am. I am, I guess. But they don't seem to notice me. The day one of them does, turns and curses me, that's when I'll stop."

Freesia started to talk again but Dora couldn't bear to listen. She stood up, pushed the door open. Freesia said, "Can I go now?"

"'Thanks for sharing, Roy,'" Roy said sarcastically, smiling at her as if he really had given her a gift.

She went downstairs to her room (past the breakfast room with the clock ticking so loud it almost hurt her ears) and sat on her bed. She looked at her phone, wanting to call someone, but who?

There was no one.

It was quiet upstairs. The neighbor hadn't been replaced yet.

When she lay down, though, she felt her ears buzz as if there was conversation going on right under her nose but she couldn't hear it. The room felt busy, buzzy, and she pulled her pillow over her head to try to make a cocoon for herself.

THIRD DAY
THURSDAY
NIGHT

Her painful bladder told her she need to go to the toilet, so she did. Almost went barefoot but the cold lino felt slimy underfoot so she slipped shoes on.

Blessed relief of pissing. Then pleasure of washing hands in warm water. She noticed that the bathroom mirror was made out of a porthole. How had she not noticed that before? She wondered if it was from the wreck and if Roy had stolen it or someone else had stolen it for him.

The hallway was dark (it was always dark, even on days that were sunny and bright) except for the glow that came from the small lounge room on the other side of the foyer. She'd never been in there but the glow, the sense of warmth, drew her there now. Someone must have left the light on. What she'd seen upstairs in Freesia's room was still with her (*that's mine*) but it was fading, like the memory of pain. The faint memory of childbirth.

The house was quiet. Everyone was out or asleep. It was different at night. The atmosphere changed. All she heard was snoring, if she stuck her head in the stairwell. *And,* she thought, *Roy's voice, asking questions.*

She walked to the lounge room thinking she'd sit for a while then turn off the light.

Inside was a man she hadn't seen before. He was white haired, very solid, dressed in an old knitted cardigan that made her think of a fisherman. He sat on a high stool and worked at a huge painting, the canvas running the length of the room and reaching halfway to the ceiling, where a bare bulb gave out bright but sometimes flickering light.

He was painting the wreck of *The Anglesea*.

"Oh," she said, because it was magnificent. It was full of ghosts and shadows and smudges that, even at a glance, she saw were deliberate.

"Oh, yourself. Pass me the turps."

A jar of the spirit sat on a table nearby and she passed it to him.

"There's a ghosty I need to move. You see him? He needs to come forward. He's too far back."

As she watched, he painted the character larger, reaching forward. It looked like the ghostly looter she'd seen talking through Freesia, she thought, but then she wondered if everything she saw would look like the looter now.

"Adding in, taking away. You have to keep at it." He rubbed at a dark gray patch with his thumb, wiped his thumb on his pants. "I thought you were a ghost at first. I can hear them coming. I know when they're about. I wasn't sure if you were real or one of them."

"I'm real and they don't exist," she said, thinking that saying it aloud might convince her.

There was a clock in this room as well, ticking gently. There were ancient paperbacks (*To Sail the Sea, The Wreck of the Tosca, My Life on the Waves*), as well as a battered Bible and *Confessions of the Dead* and incomplete boardgames and packs of cards.

There was a small step ladder to reach the high bits.

"When will you be finished?" Dora asked

"Never," he said. "There'll always be more to add. The story keeps changing. The more we hear the more we know. The more we see. You see this fella," he said, pointing at man hanging from a tree in the background. "They reckon he warned of disaster but the captain wasn't having any. Had him hanged! That there's the captain who stripped off naked and jumped overboard when the wreck happened. Here he is. I'm waiting for more on him. More information. Roy is working on it. But you know the patch down by the shore? Where no grass will grow? They say that's where he's buried. That's what they reckon. Parts of him, anyway. Bits were missing when he was found. I can't paint him till I have the story. Roy is finding out for me. Anything for art, ay? Suffering and all that. Anything for the art."

The captain was painted with a clock on his shoulder. Dora leaned close, reached a finger to it.

"Don't touch," he said. Then, "You've got a keen eye. That is our clock indeed. Indeed. Can you imagine the secrets this man must know? Can you picture the stories about him? Tough man. He hanged a lot of men. He used to call it the Dancing Legs Puppet Show. That's what we've been told."

"People love watching that stuff."

"Oh, they do. They love to watch a wreck of any kind. Human as well."

The painting was mostly beach, littered with flotsam and jetsam. A bolt of glorious purple material sat at the front, so realistic she thought she could touch it.

"Roy is a good man, you know. I wouldn't be anywhere without him. We go way back. Way back. We were in a cycling club at fifteen. Seems like an eternity ago. You couldn't get me on a bike now. I'd fall off, wouldn't I? Size of me. Roy is still a skinny bastard apart from that gut of his. He coulda been an Olympian, we used to say, if he wasn't such a fuck-up."

She'd seen Roy on his bike. He did seem different. More agile. Less repulsive.

The painter put down his brush and settled into an armchair. Without a word, he began to nod off, so she left. She'd seen enough sleeping people for one day.

~

Dora thought she'd go for another walk. She might buy some chips to bring home, or a loaf of bread. She almost felt hungry but she shouldn't, how could she be hungry with the children gone, did they die hungry? Was there anything they liked to eat? She couldn't bear that. She walked quickly (although she felt tired, a distinct lack of strength in her legs) and she walked far, trying not to think but failing.

She did buy hot chips and ate them on a park bench, looking out to sea. She felt anonymous, unknown. It was good.

~

On return, a rich, good smell filled the house. It was food cooking.

Onions, curry, she thought, and she couldn't help but look into the shared kitchen which she had not used, not even for coffee.

Mrs. Reddy, another guest, was there, along with three large pots on the massive stove. Dora had met her briefly, passing each other in the hallway.

"You're the girl in the front room, aren't you," Mrs. Reddy said. "Where all the ghosts walk. They still think that is the way into the house, foolish ghosts." She and her husband and three children had one of the bigger rooms but still Dora couldn't imagine how they all fitted in. She'd never seen husband or children and had an image of them stuffed and still, sitting up in positions Mrs. Reddy placed them in. But sometimes she couldn't imagine anyone with a living husband and children.

"I am making aloo curry and saag gosht and there is plenty. You are welcome to share. There will be daal as well."

"Oh, no, that's okay."

"Everybody else is," Larry said. He carried a massive bag of rice on his shoulder. His voice was baritone and filled the room. "I got this on special. Should last a while."

"Julia gave me lentils, so there is plenty for all."

Mrs. Reddy cooked every night for her family, simple dishes that filled the house with ordinary smells. Others burned cheese on toast, cooked two-minute noodles, opened cans of tuna. Most nights Mrs. Reddy left bowls of leftovers out, which were always gone by morning.

"Need any heavy lifting, I'm your man," Larry said to Dora. "I could lift you with one finger. Your friend Julia might be a different story. That's one hefty girl. But you? You're all class. Look at you."

Dora hated herself for not standing up for Julia. For allowing herself to be called the pretty one, to be compared.

He winked at her. He had to be in his sixties; white hair on his head and exposed on his chest, with wrinkles on his face and spots on his hands. But he still thought he had it, that he barely had to try to score with someone like Dora.

Mrs. Reddy said, "Come back in forty minutes, fifty minutes. It'll be just right then."

Roy rushed in, excited, his cheeks flushed, his step sprightly. He pulled Dora aside and whispered, "I've got a good one. He's a bloody beauty. Take a look at him," Roy said, as if he'd caught a beautiful fish. "Look at this ring." He opened his palm to show Dora, glancing around to make sure no one was looking.

It was a golden ring set with red stones.

"Gold and rubies," he said. "Only a rich man would have owned this ring. He'll have all sorts of secrets. He'll tell me where his treasure is buried. Or where the bodies are. It might be the captain's ring. He'll know some stuff. At least he'll tell me how to catch the captain. You can watch if you like."

"Why are you letting me see? Do you let anyone else?"

"Sometimes. But you're a better class of woman than we usually get in here. You actually read, for one thing."

She didn't. The book in her room was hollowed out, and she kept her money in it, and her wedding ring and her mother's diamond earrings. How could he know, though, what was in her room? And the fact he and Larry used the same term all "class" made her think they'd been talking about her.

"So, Mrs. Reddy," he said. "Rent's due."

"I'm feeding your tenants, Mr. Roy," she said, a crawling, begging tone in her voice. "You see? I'm saving you from feeding them."

"That's okay, Mrs. Reddy. You just need a good sleep. That's all. Then we won't worry about the rent."

She shook her head.

"One of the kids, then? Your son is ten, isn't he? He could do with a good sleep."

"No, no. I need the sleep. I do."

"After dinner, ay? Can't let all this good food go to waste."

∽

Dinner was delicious. Dora didn't think she'd eaten a better meal but then no one had cooked for her for a very long time.

Mrs. Reddy's room was filled with her family so, after she'd finished her meal, Roy led her to one of the vacant rooms. It was near the top of the house and at the front, so it was warmer and lighter than some of the others. There were signs that someone had cared at this stage of the house, because the wallpaper was brocade and well-placed and the light fittings not cheap and nasty.

This room smelled very strongly of cheap lilac air freshener. Dora smelled this each morning on awakening.

The doctor came in. "How'd you sleep, Dora?" he said. His smile was too friendly, too knowing, from a man she'd barely spoken too. "Hello, Mrs. Reddy. Let's get you settled, ay?"

He pushed up the sleeve of her shirt and injected something into her arm. "Sleep easy, dear lady."

She whimpered once then fell asleep.

"I'm hoping it's the captain. I'll ask him where he's hid the gold."

It took a while this time. Dora was comfortable in an armchair and dozing off when she heard "Tell her I love her. Tell her I care. Tell her I didn't do it not at sea nor on ground. Tell her I love her." She saw the shadow, the ghost, of a tall man, his hair a wild mop on his head.

"I hate these fucken ones," Roy said. "Are you the captain?"

"I'm not the captain. I'm the man he wished he was. More man than he'd ever be."

"Still," Roy said. "You've got a love story to tell. Let me hear it."

And the ghost told a broken-hearted love story that made Dora cry. "When you first fall in love you imagine it will stay that way forever. Every breath she exhales you want to inhale. Every step she takes you want to cup her heel to protect it from the hard earth. You embark on a journey together, seeking your fortune, knowing that simply being together is fortune enough. But then her head is turned by the powerful man. Her head is turned by wealth and charm and all you are is the man downstairs, without skill. All you are is strong and kind and loving and all she wants is a better name. She calls your name at the last, though. As she drowns at sea. As you reach for her to draw her to safety you see his ring on her finger and so you just let . . .

her . . .

sink."

"This'll sell well," Roy said. "Especially as this was the room where our very own Romeo and Juliet died a few years back. Romance abounds!"

Dora was so affected by the story she didn't respond.

Roy said, "I'm not kidding. They were only kids. Thirteen and fourteen. Tragic, ay? She had a single mum, he was living with his 'uncle.' This is no place for kids. Anyone'll tell you that."

"Can I go now?" the ghost said.

"No, you bloody can't. These kids; no one knows who gave them the drugs, but I do. I'm not telling." Roy tapped the side of his nose. "Terrible story. Sad."

"Can't I go?" the ghost said.

As if they were co-conspirators, Roy said to Dora, "These bloody ghosts love it, really. Some of them never shut up. Mr. Cox . . . you haven't met him yet. But he was on the verge of death when he came to us. Literally on his last legs, last breath, ready to pop the mortal coil. But then our good doctor helped him sleep, and we heard him talk, and there you go."

"So he's still alive?"

"Mr. Cox? Lives on the third floor. Comes down for Sunday dinner, six p.m. on the dot if you want to take a look at him. He's pretty quiet. Don't get much out of him unless he's asleep. Then he's very chatty."

Dora left them after a while. The painter was at work downstairs and he asked her what had happened and he painted as she spoke, adding details she'd heard Freesia speak.

FOURTH DAY
FRIDAY
BREAKFAST

There were dreams of strangers. Things long past. She woke with a sore throat, as if she'd been talking all night.

~

"How'd you sleep?" Roy asked. The day always started with that question. Sometimes she answered it three or four times.

"Okay. I actually slept, I think, which is unusual."

"You get addicted to the sleep here. Wait and see."

Dora took a plate. "This place is huge, isn't it? Does it belong to some rich old family?"

"It's mine, actually. A gambling debt paid off." Quietly, he said to her, "Friend and I slept on the beach, five years ago. Just after he got let out of prison. I was already living here, had done for what, ten years? But he wanted to sleep without any walls around him. Down there, where the ghosts are. My friend talked in his sleep and I swear, he told me where the deeds were. Place was abandoned before that. It's been mine ever since."

"What about your friend? Didn't he want part of it?"

He indicated the painter. "He didn't want it. I let him stay here for free. Do what he likes. He's got the good deal out of it. None of the stress, all of the gain."

At breakfast the painter blinked constantly, squinted, his fingers pinched knife and fork as if they were paintbrushes. He talked about nothing but his method, the brilliance of it. "No big deal," he said, but answered almost every statement, every hello and goodbye, with "I'm glad you asked that," as if practicing for an interview.

"How'd you sleep?" Dora asked him.

"Oh, I sleep very little. Two hour bursts in the chair where I fell. You saw me."

"Have you seen his painting? Incredible. Five years he's been at it. Stroke by stroke by stroke," Roy said. "What a talent! Pure genius! Should be famous, probably will be once he's dead. You watch, they'll knock this place down in order to get at his work of art."

Roy winked and Dora realized to her horror that he was being cruel.

"You've been friends a long time."

"Cycling club together, believe it or not. Then he goes and kills a girl, gets locked up."

"You got forty years free to live a life, ya cunt. Did you use those forty years, mate? Or didja let 'em slip by with the bottle and the needle? You coulda done that locked up," the painter said.

"You know I used them, Al. I used them better than you would of."

"Yeah, well."

The painter said that the spirit of the girl he'd killed came to him and told him he needed to confess, so he did. He said he'd paid his debt "and that's more than I can say for some." He said he learned how to paint in prison and that it was the best thing to happen to him. "Gives me focus, right? Not like this bastard, ay. Coulda been something, never was. Aspiring Olympic cyclist, that's the best we can call him."

"Not my fault, and there's nothing wrong with being aspiring," Roy said with a shrug, a grin. "My sick mother."

"Today it's your sick mother!" Larry called out. "Yesterday you survived colon cancer. Last week you reckoned you had a family to support."

"It's always something," the painter said.

"I had a traumatic incident when I was just a kiddie," Roy said. "I'm not saying what. But let me tell you. A man with two faces is a man to be feared, that's what I reckon."

Dora had seen his two sides, the neat, handsome one and the dirty, pathetic one.

"All that was a long time ago." He seemed to like talking about himself over breakfast, when he had them captive.

"You know what's not a long time ago?" Larry said. "The stink in my room. Go easy on pumping the air freshener willya, mate? My room stinks of lilac."

"Need to keep the rooms fresh," Roy said. "Each one has had a death in it. As you know."

Dora realized he had been opening their doors and spraying the stuff in. She'd smelled it, too.

"If I don't spray every day the smell gets on top of me. Of you, too. Look, at least you've got a roof over your heads. Don't know what you're whining about."

"You don't have to treat us like dogs, and we don't have to be grateful," Larry said.

"You can always live in your car. Or out on the street."

"I couldn't sleep in a car," Julia said.

"You couldn't fit in a car," Roy said. Larry laughed the loudest at that one.

The doctor said, "I can help you sleep anywhere. You know I'm a whizz with sleep."

Julia shook her head. "Give me a chance to recover from the last one."

"Sleep would be nice," Dora said.

"Sleep is nice," the doctor said. "I find it hard myself. Never been able to sleep. Well. Not since my sister went missing. You know? You blame yourself." His hair was dyed red and washed out.

"Who can sleep in this place? Talking, talking, all night long. I can't sleep," Julia said.

"You are asleep, and you're the one talking," the doctor said. "Not being able to sleep is a terrible thing. People don't understand if sleep comes easy for them. My mother always slept. Got pissed and slept for hours. Days. She'd do it in the afternoon so we'd get home to a cold dark house and no food. We ate a lot of tinned soup. We never slept well, my brothers and me. You never knew when she'd wake up and she'd want us up at the same time. She'd come in and stare at us until we woke up. Stand by the bed just staring. Unless she got sick of waiting, then you'd wake up with a slap in the face. A bloody nose. And she'd say, *Oh, no a bloody nose! You'd better get up, and all of us had to. What I'm looking for is peaceful sleep for all.*

You can't do damage when you're asleep. You can't think about your own guilt. You fight the monsters you know."

"You can't blame yourself, mate. You were only seven," the painter said.

"Yeah, well. I just want it to be over with. I wish we'd found her. There is nothing more painful that what we went through. What we're going through. "

Dora said, "But you were only seven. You did nothing wrong. None of your choices made it happen. Mine did. My own pathetic monster hunting, my pathetic . . ."

"It probably wasn't your fault," Julia said, but she didn't look at Dora and Dora thought: *they know, they know what I did* and she felt her heart pounding so hard she thought it would break. She was dizzy, her fingers tingled and she broke out in a cold sweat.

She clutched her chest.

"She's having a heart attack!" Julia said. The doctor washed his hands at the sink and kneeled next to Dora.

"It's a panic attack. It'll be okay. Don't worry. I'll help you sleep," and he took her arm.

His fingers were like ice.

He gave her a bottle of pills, saying, "Take two as required and see me if pain persists." He laughed, as if it wasn't a joke he must have made a dozen times.

FIFTH DAY
SATURDAY
BREAKFAST

Dora didn't know what the doctor had given her but when she woke up she felt calm, able to be with people.

~

Mrs. Reddy was at breakfast without her family. She sat in the corner, eating cereal that was placed before her, drinking coffee. The doctor sat with her, rising to wash his hands every few minutes.

"She's a bit tired still. Family are having a break away. How'd you sleep, Mrs. Reddy?" the doctor asked her.

Her mouth was droopy and her eyes dull.

"How are you feeling, Dora? After your panic attack? We've all been there. You can tell us about it if you want," Julia said. "You know it's good to talk."

"You just want to hear another sad story," Larry said. "You're a fucken pariah."

"We all love sad stories," Julia said.

Dora said, "I don't know if you've been married, or in a long-term relationship . . ." In the breakfast room all the cutlery was silent. "I . . . but you know when it starts out, you can't imagine it being over. Like a friendship, like you know your friend from high school, who you think will be your friend forever? And they fade away and you think of them every now and then till you don't. Long term relationships you start in love but you end up hating each other. He fucked around on me which makes him an arse-hole. Not a monster. But if I thought of him as a monster I could pretend he was evil, that I never loved a monster. I told my kids he was evil, didn't I? Told them so many stories about how awful he was they didn't trust him."

Luke came and sat with her. She'd imagined his past by now, wondered what it was he'd done to make him want to live here. It wasn't what he'd seen, it was what he'd done. She was sure.

"Tell us about it," he said. He put his hand on hers.

"I wrote a story about it," she said. "This isn't my story. This is made up."

No one told her that a safe place could be dangerous too.

When she was five, her bedroom was safe if she pushed her chair against the door. Her sister could not get in to pinch pinch pinch.

But you couldn't trust safety. Like that man you thought you loved. Loved you. How quickly he turned.

When she was twenty-five, she could lock herself in the toilet, stuff toilet paper in her mouth and scream scream scream, then she would be safe from hurting the children, safe from taking up the cord from her electric frypan and swinging it around like a lariat, spinning it against the flesh of those nagging, smelly children who trusted her because she was Mummy.

"Don't forget your lunches," she says to her children, her two little girls.

She dropped the children at school and tried to decide what to do for the day. The phone rang. She knew it was Derek. He called every day at 12:15, when his boss went to lunch.

"Stop harassing me, Derek," she said, her words clear, her vowels round. "Leave us alone."

"I want to see the girls," he said. "You have to let me see them."

"Don't threaten me. You don't scare me anymore. And leave the kids alone, you monster."

"I'm not threatening. Please. I just want to see them. Make sure they're okay."

She hung up on him.

The girls were allowed to walk home from school, together. She'd walked it with them a dozen times, pointing out the house with the Safe House sign on it. The house that had been checked, that would be safe for them to run to if there was danger.

If a monster came for them.

"Yes, we know," said the oldest. She was placid, unhurried. "They told us at school. If there's a stranger or you're scared, go to that house."

"And?" she said.

The girl shrugged. "And if Daddy tries to kidnap you," she said. "Because if you see Daddy, you should run as fast as you can. Daddy has long teeth, sharp, he hides them with other teeth. He has a sharp knife, he told me he wants to see your insides. He wants to keep you locked away forever."

She reminded them every day. Daddy was evil.

Eventually they believed her.

She made some chocolate spread sandwiches at 3:15, poured some milk, and waited, sitting high on a kitchen stool, for her children to return from school. She would wait until their mouths were full then ask them about their nightmares.

"Hello, my little darlings," she would say.

Her children never come home.

Derek called her at four p.m. "Why did the kids run away from me? What have you told them?"

She felt icicles in her brain, a knife in her heart. "What have you done with them? Where are they?"

"They ran away from me, I just said. Up the pathway. By the time I drove around they were gone."

The pathway led to the Safe House and she felt a sense of relief.

"They haven't come home," she said. They didn't speak. She knew, admitted, suddenly and clearly, that Derek was not a bad man.

"I think I know where they might be," she said.

"I'm coming over," he said.

The girls were not at the Safe House but they'd been there; their killer even taunted Derek, goaded him and made it so clear what had happened that on the spot Derek became a killer himself.

He said he didn't regret it, not for a minute. Even though every minute of his life was spent behind bars now.

She is safe now, in the warm house of her body. All the torrents and currents are hers, and she always knows when she is about to cry.

Nobody spoke for a few moments. Nobody moved.

Then Freesia said, "Did they die?"

She didn't answer. She couldn't.

"Your ex must really fucken hate you," Larry said.

They all started to eat. "That's why I'm here. I deserve this shit hole," Dora said.

"Hey!" Roy said. He seemed truly offended. "This place isn't that bad," but it was, really; the grime, the size of the rooms, the food. All of them were there as a last resort. "We do our best," Roy said.

Julia said, "Half of us are here because we think we deserve it. But if we really wanted to suffer we'd be out on the streets. So we're weak and pathetic, really."

Then Freesia said, "All men are monsters. You were right. You tried to keep them safe. You kept them safe from the monster you know. You can't know about them all." She seemed tireder, sadder, and she had a cold that caused her to sniff constantly.

"He wasn't really a monster. He just didn't love me enough. He was the only boyfriend I'd had. The only man."

"Seriously?" Luke said. She wondered if she was using sex with him to make her feel wanted. She didn't understand you can say "no."

Freesia said, "If you thought it, it was for a reason. It wasn't all your imagination. Your anxieties."

"He wasn't a monster, though. I made them run to a monster."

But Freesia had already lost interest and was flirting with the doctor. She was keen on Luke too. She was keen on all the men. She was tiny, her teeth bad, with her mouth shut her cheeks caved in a bit. She had pictures of herself as a young girl. *Even then she looked damaged*, Dora thought. She looked at herself in the mirror and understood that no one could tell, looking at her. She was soft. She'd had so few traumas in her life.

It was true that her husband had affairs. He slept around. He became more and more obvious as time went on and that made her less and less attracted to him and that made him go further and further afield, and closer, too, with her best friend falling into his arms.

Luke was her first after him. He assumed she was something else, someone not terrified, someone sexy, sensual, who slept with strangers because she wanted to. It's not her but it could be her.

The painter said, "That bloke will be haunted by your little girls, wherever he is. They'll come to him, they'll say their names. That's what happened to me. I didn't even mean to kill that poor girl but it doesn't mean she left me alone. *Save me save me save me confess.* Feeling sorry for herself. Don't you hate self-pity? Like that bitch up there."

He jerked a thumb at the ceiling. "She's up there using her disability as an excuse. It sickens me." Dora wondered who he was talking about but at the same time didn't want to know.

"She really can't look after herself anymore," the doctor said, washing his hands. "I'm pretty sure she'd rather be able to look after herself. She's terrified of baths, you know. Water of all kinds. We have to put her to sleep to wash her."

"She's one of my best girls," Roy said.

"Poor woman was badly burned in the last place she lived. The only place she finds peace is asleep. So we help her out."

Dora checked her phone but no one had called her. She wondered if they thought differently about her but knew that none of them really cared.

She watched Luke, and he looked back at her. "Come visit," he whispered in her ear.

～

On his floor there was thick, old carpet in the hallway. She had shoes on but wondered what it would feel like on bare feet. It looked sticky and dirty.

Luke was happy to see her, it seemed. He squeezed her arse, gave her a drink, told her he needed a shower and drew her in with him. She hadn't done it like that before; her ex-husband had been a very private person about the bathroom.

～

They sat wrapped in towels, looking out over the beach. Dora thought she could hear a murmuring through the wall. Crying, interspersed with periods of silence.

"Who's next door?"

"That poor woman. I think the nurse is the only one who sees her. She looks pretty bad. She used to live in a group home but someone dropped her in a hot bath. Her legs never worked but now they're fucking terrifying. We've all seen them. Everyone sneaks in for a look. You can. Door is never locked. Someone knocked the lock off coz he wanted to get a look at her. Don't worry," he said, raising his hands, "That guy's gone. Killed himself."

She'd heard this quite a lot since she'd moved in. There were memorials around the building for dead tenants. Murder, suicide, natural causes. Small urns, paintings, statues, mostly with a sea motif, and when she looked closely she could see a name and a date.

"Funny thing is, she's always smiling. Makes it even freakier, to be honest."

~

Dora felt wide awake, wired by coffee and pills the doctor had given her to make her feel better. She paused to listen at the burned woman's room.

Dora stared in. The woman was in bed, covers thrown off, nightgown pushed up over her breasts. Her legs were terrifying; scarred, flaking, dark brown in some places as if the flesh had rotted. Yet she was smiling.

Dora tugged the nightgown down, straightening it over her knees and her shins.

She went back to her room. Things had been disturbed in there, she was sure.

"Roy!" she called out. She didn't like to go into his office. "Someone's been at my room."

He came and looked in. "There are always thefts. We all learn to keep little of value in our rooms. Most people here, all we own are memories. No one can steal those. They are ours and we're the ones in control of them. Anything missing?"

"I don't think so."

"You're lucky, then. The probably just wanted to sniff your bedsheets." He was so matter of fact about this she was sure it was him.

"Can I have clean sheets then?"

"On Monday."

"Please." She thought she'd cry. Stupidly, she thought she'd cry if she didn't have clean sheets.

"All right. But you owe me."

~

The new sheets smelled musty but at least she knew she was the first to sleep in them. She curled up in bed and thought of how he would ask her to repay this debt.

She felt them walking over her in the dark, those old ghosts marching to a place that no longer existed.

FIFTH DAY
SATURDAY
NIGHT

Dora knew she should get ready. She knew they were gathering for the Ship Wreck party Luke had told her about. She wished he'd said he'd go with her, knock on her door, and they'd arrive together. But he didn't.

She had nothing to wear. She had no idea what the others would wear, although Freesia was always Freesia and would dress in layers.

She looked at her clothing hanging on the hooks on the old front door as if something would magically appear there. But it didn't. A pair of old jeans, a pale blue T-shirt with nothing on it, a thin gray cardigan. She didn't want to be that person. She wanted to be THIS Dora, the one who lived in the front room and who fitted in.

She curled up in her bed until past the time they were gathering.

A knock at her door gave her hope, but it wasn't Luke. It was Roy. He had washed his hair and slicked it back, and he smiled with his mouth closed so she couldn't see his bad teeth.

"Coming along? The others are having a get-together. All welcome. All welcome in this place."

"I haven't got anything to wear," Dora said.

She knew it sounded ridiculous but he said, "I can help you there! Come on."

He led her to his office. She hadn't seen inside before. It was larger than she'd expected, neat, but crammed full of nautical things. Ships in bottles, wheels, pictures of shipwrecks, thick rope.

He moved a pile of brass fittings off a large trunk, *Property of S. Fisher*, and opened it.

Inside were clothes and shoes. "People always leave stuff behind," he said. "What's mine is yours, yours mine, ours theirs . . ." he stopped, as if realizing he was babbling, and wiped a streak of saliva from his chin.

Dora picked out a pair of white pants, a red-striped shirt, some shoes that looked like waves.

"Little Cabin Boy," Roy said.

~

They all sat drinking together on the front veranda. Dora pretended she was someone else, the sort of person who hung out at parties. She'd always hidden behind other people. Parents, friends, husband, kids. It was never *her* being presented but the daughter, friend, wife, mother.

Even here, really, she was Front Room Dora. Not herself, not by a long shot.

She had little to say but it didn't matter. People had brought bottles. She had very little with her in the car but she had taken two cases of wine that had been delivered. Her ex-husband had signed up for the service years earlier and she kept accepting the wine he continued to pay for, automatic payment. He didn't really have access to banks where he was.

She arrived with two bottles and they cheered her. "Welcome to the Ship Wreck!" She felt important for a moment.

She drank more wine than she usually did. She felt lighter as her brain numbed; there were moments when she actually laughed. Freesia sat at Luke's feet, leaning up against him rubbing his shins. He didn't seem to notice, or perhaps he thought she was a cat or a dog sitting there loyally. Dora expected him to pat Freesia on the head.

Larry showed off, lifting furniture like the massive table that had come off the ship. She felt as if they were on a ship. Roy had built furniture out of the wreckage and you could almost imagine you were out at sea.

Dora laughed. Felt Larry's muscles. "You are all class," he said. Up close he smelled of beer, of old man. His hair unwashed. He was what she deserved. Nothing more.

Luke stood up then, and Freesia fell forward dramatically. No one noticed. He said, "She is class, all right. Way out of yours, mate," and he put his arm around Dora, kissed her cheek, got her another wine.

Dora gave Larry a look, an "oh well" kind of look she hoped would keep him interested.

Someone called for pizza, the cheap and nasty kind they could all afford. Pizza was usually on her no go list. Anything the girls used to eat was on that list. She'd cook three meals sometimes, adult and two different ones for the children.

She didn't like eating with others. So many foods gave her pause, made her think. The foods the girls had loved, the foods they'd hated.

"I'm not hungry," Julia said, and Larry snorted.

"She's probably eaten two pizzas before she even got here," he said.

"Eat something then you can sleep again," the doctor said. "When you sleep, you have an appetite. It's one of those things."

"I'd like to sleep," Dora said. "For days."

Someone had brought some custard tarts he'd bought from the bakery, days old, cheap. The girls had never had a custard tart so Dora took one but they were very well past safe eating. It tasted moldy, like off milk, and the filling was curdled.

Not even people as desperate as they were could eat them.

Mr. Cox was there but no one spoke to him. It was the first time Dora had seen him in the flesh. He was a very old man. *Ninety or more,* she thought. He sat straight in the swing chair and quietly drank a soft drink from a glass. He looked out to the water. Back and forth, back and forth, swinging gently.

"Looking for a dolphin?" Freesia asked him.

"Always keep an eye out. Lifesaver family, mine; never drink. You never know when you'll be called to rescue and you couldn't live with yourself if someone died because you'd had a drink."

He said that if you feel guilt about someone and they die, you want your grief to be over. For it to go away. But if you loved them and you don't feel guilt, the grief is important to you.

"Turn a blind eye. Best way to get through life is to turn a blind eye," he said.

Dora wondered if this was part of his family history. If he was speaking family guilt, if he'd lost someone. He was once a hero although he wouldn't admit it. His country was close to the water and some of his people still lived there, although the land was long ago taken from them. He told Dora he remembered stories of rescue, but his name wasn't in the history books, nor those of his brothers who gave their lives saving people. "It's always the other fella," he said. "Doesn't bother me. I didn't do it for the thanks," but this life meant he didn't really prepare for anything else. Back and forth, back and forth.

"We go way back, Mr. Cox, don't we? Me and you and our artist friend," Roy said.

"You were a good boy then."

"I'm good now!" Roy said. "Can't say otherwise."

Dora wondered why a man like Mr. Cox, who really did seem to be a good man, would have anything to do with Roy.

Soon, there was a moment's silence. Three minutes, when the clock through the window, sitting in the breakfast room, ticked loudly, and that was all they could hear. Dora checked her phone: three minutes to midnight.

When they started speaking again, Larry said, "Who's missing? Who's asleep?"

Dora realized that Roy wasn't with them. "Roy?" she said, and the looks they gave her made her realize she'd misunderstood something.

"It's Mrs. Reddy again. She's good. She's one of his best girls," Larry said. He stood looking down over the veranda. Most of the view was blocked by bushes and trees but there was a small part of the path to the coast visible in the moonlight. He pointed. "They're trekking up tonight."

Dora stood beside him. She could see them too, ghostly figures trudging up the hill.

"Who wants a drink?" Luke said. "Who wants a fucking drink?"

They all did.

Dora sat beside him. The music strumming gently, beautiful songs, and when she leaned close to Luke she thought she heard a voice, a murmuring, coming from him but his lips weren't moving. She smelled salt, like over-salted fish and chips or pasta water when she remembered to put the salt in.

"Is that Roy pumping smells at us again?" she said.

"You're sniffing a ghost," Larry said. "That's what you can smell."

She pushed at Luke, trying to rouse him, but Larry pulled her to her feet and had her dance with him, slow dancing to the music. He was so big, so tall, she felt enclosed by him, comforted. He was her father in that moment, and she was five or six, dancing at someone's wedding, and she'd never felt safer.

Julia tugged her arm. "He's a sleaze, Dora. Just . . . look at him. He's ancient."

"Fuck off you fat cunt," Larry said.

"I know I'm fat."

"You're not," Dora said.

"I am. When you say I'm not you're lying. Everyone does it." She sank into an armchair that was cat-damaged, water-damaged, very soft. She seemed to sink farther and farther into it as if it was swallowing her.

"You're like a fucken whale," Larry said.

"Larry," Dora said, but so quiet no one heard.

Julia said, "Did you ever think we might be living in the belly of a whale? All forgotten. And the whale keeps us drugged and pain-free while he digests us one by one."

"Is that why I've got a pain in my gut?" Larry said.

"Is that why everything tastes of fish?" Freesia said.

"Is that why you've all got salt for blood?" the doctor said, all of them joking.

Dora touched the walls near her, and they felt soft. The boards of the veranda, too, felt soft, and there was a strong smell of fish in the air.

"Do you think?" she said Larry. "Do you really think?"

"Stop freaking me out!" Julia said. "It's too creepy to think about."

Larry started moving the heavy furniture about again. His strength was the last thing he had left. He drank four bottles of beer in an hour, then went inside to watch a rugby game on the TV in the common room, and came back drunker. He was aggressive, ready to be dismissed, ignored. He must have always had people avoiding him. He was inappropriate when talking about women. Had he always been this way or had he lost his inner voice?

He came back argumentative, so when he saw Luke talking to Dora he started a fight about where the table should sit.

Dora had noticed that arguments happen to scale. It all means a lot to the people involved, regardless of monetary value. In prison it's cigarettes, juice, drugs. For the wealthy, its actual properties. In this place, it was personal time, and it was the good chair, and maybe the best room. In a wealthy neighborhood the stakes appeared to be higher but really the fury/envy/greed was the same.

Luke wasn't interested in the argument. He staggered inside and some of the others started to disperse, too.

Julia slumped in her chair. Very drunk. Dora and Larry and the doctor helped her to her bed.

Larry groped at her, copping a feel.

At her door, Larry said, "I got it from here."

Dora said, "No, don't worry. I'll sit with her. I'll be with her." She knew what he had in mind and she wasn't letting that happen.

He snarled at her; there was no other description for it.

Julia's room was larger than hers and had a window. The bed was sunken, as if broken, but it looked as if it had an extra mattress. There was one chair in the room, laden down with clothes, and there was a smell of fake cheese, like Cheetos or Cheezels. She had a shelf of books: Roy's books and a lot of true crime.

Dora sat with her. The doctor said, "We'll have to watch she doesn't vomit. She'll choke on it."

So they propped her on her side.

Before long she started to talk. "Should I call Roy?" Dora said.

"Fuck Roy. He doesn't have to listen to everything. You stay with her, listen if you want. I'm going to bed. She's not going to cark it tonight."

Julia made choking noises, raised her hands to her neck. "Can't breathe, can't breathe," the voice said. Squatting on the bed beside Julia, then straddling her, was a young man. Handsome, almost, if something she could barely see could be handsome. He leant over Julia, pressed his lips to her ear.

"You'd call it murderous rage, wouldn't you? If it was one of us done it. If it's him he says 'justified.' Me arse is still sore, I swear and as for me neck."

"Is it the captain?" Dora asked. "Where is he?"

"Saved himself, didn't he. That's him. If I saw him now he'd be sorry. And his daughter."

His voice was bitter, vindictive, helpless.

Then he said, "Tell my Linda Jane I love her."

"Why do you keep coming? Why don't you go somewhere else?"

"We were told to go up the hill. Make it up the hill, to the light on the hill, and everything will be all right."

They were still trying to make it up the hill, to the false lights Roy had hanging on the front veranda.

She didn't tell him his loved one was long dead.

The ghost stretched his hands out, broken fingers bent sideways. He said, "It's cold. This water. Wouldn't my mum be proud, here I am staying afloat. Let her know. Look at me, Mum, I'm swimming. I'm one of those types now. Tell her not to look at my back but if she does tell her it wasn't my fault, I really didn't do the thing he said I did. Fifty lashes I took. You'd be proud, Mum, I took them like a man. I cried the other time, though, when he made me the lady. He said the dress was nice but it felt like wearing a dead woman's skin. We cursed him, that captain, to be at the end of his line."

He said, "Can I go now?"

SIXTH DAY
SUNDAY
BREAKFAST

Sleep was supposed to be restorative but Dora woke feeling worse. Exhausted, her throat sore as if she's been talking all night.

Her jaw ached from laughing the night before.

She felt a deep sense of despair, as if in her dreams she lived out a different life, one even darker and sadder.

Luke had left a note under her door so she went upstairs and knocked on his door. There was no answer.

The burned woman's door was open. It was always open. Peering in, Dora saw her skirt was raised up again, exposing her bush, her scarred legs. She was in a deep sleep, lips murmuring. Dora heard "Is there any parsley for the sauce? Cook sent me. Cook did. Cook's long gone now. I know that, here's me looking for parsley. I can't see what's next. I keep looking and looking but there's nothing there."

Dora laughed.

"Shh," she heard and she spun to see Roy in the corner, crouched down, with a microphone in his hands. He put his fingers to his lips, but he whispered "You can play with yourself if you like. Some people can't help it," and she was ashamed to realize that she did feel aroused. That was more thinking about Luke, though.

Not this.

Not this woman talking in the voice of someone long dead.

"Who are you?" Dora asked her, but there was no answer.

The woman stopped talking soon after and Roy nodded. He jerked his head to indicate they should leave. In the hallway he said, "You were a very good conduit last night."

This would account for her sore throat, and she felt a blank space in her head as if she'd had a big night and was suffering an alcohol blackout. Certainly she'd had enough to drink to make that possible.

"Who was it?" she asked. "What did they say?"

"A little girl. She mostly spoke about trying to find her mother, but there was mention of the captain, too. I need the captain. He's the last bit of the puzzle. I need him to fill in the blanks. Finish the story. Your little girl said he had very pink skin so how would she know that? That's what I want to know. She said he was pink like a little piggy."

Dora smelled salt, felt a warmth pass her by.

"What happens to the ghosts once their secret is told? Can they leave?"

Roy said, "Except no one's story's ever finished. It's like his painting. It changes, is added to. The more we know, the more it changes. That's why some of them keep coming back. Come on, now. Breakfast."

As they walked Dora thought, *we should stop this. If I can stop Larry from raping Julia, I can stop this.*

~

The thing with this place was that no one missed breakfast no matter how they felt. Unless they were in deep sleep. Because for a lot of them it was the only meal for the day.

So most of them were there. The room felt full, overfull, as if there were people there she couldn't see. But they were there; hungover, feeling unwell, but it was more than that. They'd all slept, deep, deep sleeps.

Larry was dressed in a suit. "He always wears it on Sundays," Roy said. "Sometimes he even goes to church."

They could see the congregation gathering at the Anglican church across the road. They watched and laughed at the people arriving in their neat clothes with their stitched up lives.

"Our guests all head to church on Sundays. Down the hill. Then I drag 'em back up again, or they come of their own accord," Roy said as if this was something to be proud of.

For some of these church-goers, Sunday was their only day of communicating with others.

"They look kind," Dora said, but she'd known people like this.

"Remember when that guy from the third floor fell over out there? Literally on the road? They ignored him."

"They fucken didn't," Larry said. "One of them came over to tell us. How do you think he got inside? I carried him once they told me."

"You notice they assumed he was one of ours. Typical."

"He was, wasn't he? So they were right."

Dora felt the atmosphere pressing down on her. It was like being in a sauna, the air hot and thick and hard to breathe.

She went back to her room, thinking how lucky she was that she could go back to sleep now. No one wanted anything from her. No one cared if she slept or not.

~

Dora heard a voice that sounded like her mother's, and she couldn't breathe, the tears came so hard and fast. She listened at the window, it wasn't her mother but a lady like her, arguing with a man who must be her husband, *no we can't park behind, that's not the entrance I told you*, their voices fading.

They made such a fuss arriving half the rooming house were there to watch them walk through the gate, a middle-aged couple, well-dressed, loud.

"I'm Trevor. Gray nomad at large." *One of those funny men*, Dora thought.

"Never shuts up," his wife said. "Even talks in his sleep."

"Good sleeper, is he?" Roy asked

"You must be the team. The gang. The Mob. Oops!" Trevor said, this last as he noticed Mr. Cox. "Sorry, mate. No mob here, only us whiteys—oops, there I go again," he said. "This is my wife, Val."

Trevor was handsome in an immature way. Quite short, bouncy so he seemed like a little dog. Silver hair, few wrinkles, smooth skin. Blue eyes. He was too kind for them to be piercing, but they were very clear.

The woman had high heels and deep rich red hair.

"*Costs me a fortune,*" she confided to Dora later. "*But I hate the color from a box. Looks so tacky.*"

"*I can tell you use a good brand,*" Dora said. *That was not a salon color, no way.*

Roy invited them to have a seat on the veranda. "Freesia will make us all a cuppa, won't you, Freesia? You'll like her. She's very helpful," he said. "We get a lot of gray nomads stopping on their journeys around the country."

Val said, "I used to be gray. My late husband said I should age gracefully. I say bugger that."

"Late husband?"

"Trevor's my new one!"

"She traded up," Trevor said.

Roy said, "It's not unheard of for an old bastard to die suddenly."

"He was sixty-seven! Left me with a fair bit in the bank at least. His retirement fund. Some life insurance. And the safe. This bloody safe I didn't even know we had, hidden in the boot of the car."

"What was in it?" As annoying as Dora found the woman, she told a good story.

"I don't know, do I? Can't get the bloody thing open. Took it to a locksmith and he said we'd have to blow it open. But we don't want to blow up the contents is the problem."

"Problem all right," Roy said. "What do you keep with you in a life on the road? What is precious?"

"Memories. But they are so untrustworthy. That's why we need items, to help keep the stories straight. I want to know what he kept."

"We could just not," Trevor said.

Freesia arrived with a tray of old mugs and teabags. She wasn't pleased, but Roy gave her a wink. Dora wondered if this meant she wouldn't have to sleep with the ghosts that night.

"We're here because we met someone who told us you can talk to ghosts. This friend of mine told me about this weird thing, how he came here with his boyfriend and caught him talking in his sleep. But it wasn't him. It was the cabin boy from that shipwreck. Coming through."

Trevor shook his head. "She's always on about it." He kissed her cheek. "Gorgeous, isn't she?"

Dora thought: *never before married, he can't believe his luck now. He's not lonely anymore. But he's cute and seems reasonably intelligent. So what? Why?*

"Word is getting out, I guess. That we talk to the ghosts of the shipwreck. This place is like a wine bar for ghosts. A place for conversation. Ghosts are like the homeless and the lonely. I like the homeless. They'll talk to anyone. And they sleep easy. The lonely? Depends on how long they've been lonely for. If it's been too long, they've forgotten how to speak."

"I wondered if you'd had luck talking to anyone who wasn't in the shipwreck?"

"They didn't all drown. Some bled to death, some starved or died of thirst. You can tell by the state they're in."

"It's the safe, see. My husband's safe." She didn't seem to mind showing off her cleavage, which was tanned. She caught Dora staring at it. "Don't mind the topless sunbathing. I know they say it'll give me cancer, but I don't know about that. When you've seen your husband drop dead like mine did, you learn to live a little. One minute he's reaching up above the sink into his booze cupboard, next minute he's flat out. Took me a while to realize what was up. And we were miles from anywhere. So far away. I had to drive the bloody caravan . . ."

"She hates driving the caravan," Trevor said.

". . . I had to drive for about two hours before I saw a single person. Phones didn't work out there and I wasn't going to get on the radio and let every pervert in the vicinity know I was a woman on my own."

Roy stood beside her, rubbing his hands together. He said, "You'd be surprised at the secrets old people bring along. I can tell you some stories, for sure."

He did, too, gossiping and making them all laugh. This was Roy at his best. Holding the interest of the room with good material. Some of them were stories Dora had heard before, others were new ones. She wondered what stories he'd tell about her once she left.

Trevor stepped up to compete with his own stories of outrageous behavior. Dora liked the way he told a story and the stories he chose. Unlike Roy, who splattergunned stories until one stuck, Trevor seemed to be more selective. She liked the rise and fall of his voice and his chest and the way his hair sat on his head. She wondered if

Luke would be jealous of the attention she was giving Trevor, but Luke was asleep, out of her vision.

Eventually, the topic returned to the dead first husband. "He actually died in the caravan?" Roy asked.

"Yes, he did. I would have sold it and got a new one but never got around to it. And the car, too. I didn't want to sell it without opening the safe. You'd think he had the crown jewels in there. But part of me doesn't want to know what's in there. You know?"

"How bad could it be?" someone said.

"Pretty fucking bad," Larry said.

"We could see if your husband will come talk to you, give you the combination. You know that combination lock test, where they ask a ghost for the combination to a safe? No one's done it yet. It'd be real proof, right? For the doubters. I don't need it. I know they're here," Roy said.

"Do they ever answer? The ghosts."

"They sometimes answer. It's often not very nice, though. Ghosts who are anchored here can be bitter, vindictive. They are bloody nasty, mostly. You'll have to be ready for that."

"I'll give you quarter of whatever's in the safe," she said.

"You don't know what's in there!" Roy seemed to find this amusing. "It could be nothing but sentimental crap."

"I'll give you actual money. A grand," Trevor said, and the deal was made.

"If we manage to call him in, do you want to be the sleeping one? Or Trevor? Or one of mine?" Roy said.

"Maybe one of yours? It'll be too odd to have my husbands merged together."

"It might work better if Trevor does it."

Val looked at Trevor, then turned to Roy and nodded.

Trevor looked slightly bewildered, as if he'd thought this was a joke. Val scrabbled in her bag and gave him a packet of cigarettes and a lighter. "Not inside," she said.

Roy said, "Do you have anything of your late husband's? Anything bodily, I mean."

"I've got his ashes."

"Perfect."

They went to the caravan. Trevor was nervous, darting back and forth, reminding Dora again of a little dog.

"He bounces around like this then he's flat-out. Seriously, he's like a puppy," Val said.

"But I'm very mature in other ways, right?" Trevor said. Dora knew she'd never get a sweet man like him. An innocent.

Roy and Val went into the caravan alone. "Have you lived here long?" Trevor said, making conversation. Dora had to count on her fingers.

"Five days!" she said, which astonished her. She'd gone into Roy's trunk and borrowed some more clothes, so she was wearing a bright wraparound dress that clung to her. Her feet were bare but she didn't mind that look. She hoped Trevor had noticed her, but she thought he hadn't. He had little interest in someone like her. She still liked him, though. He was kind, thoughtful. She'd try a different dress in the evening, especially if Luke still failed to appear.

Roy came out carrying a cigar box. "Here he is! You can all wait outside if you like. Dora, we're going to use your room. You can attend or not. It's up to you."

He led them to Dora's room. She wished she'd put her dirty underwear in the suitcase and tried to clean up ahead of them, blushing at the smell in there because there was no good air, just the smell of her. She hated the smell of herself.

Roy tucked the box of ashes under Dora's pillow. She wished there weren't dirty tissues under there.

"Who is going to be the sleeper? Dora? I'm not sure you've really made much of a contribution yet, although I know you've tried. Or Trevor? It will be an experience for you. To speak another man's words."

"Trevor," Val said, her voice thick.

Roy had called the doctor, who came dressed only in a pair of skimpy shorts. His chest hair was gray and stringy, not matching his head hair. He looked out of sorts, beside himself, as if his ghost rested just out of place.

"I was dreaming about my sister," he said.

Trevor lay down on Dora's bed. His feet stretched almost to the end and he looked good there. She wondered what it would be like to wake up next to him.

Only Trevor and the doctor were actually in the room, with Roy, Val, and Dora crowded outside.

"Your room is smaller than my caravan bedroom," Val said. "You're nuts to stay here."

Dora felt tears prick her eyes. She didn't think she should have to justify herself to this stranger.

"All settled?" Roy said. The doctor folded up Trevor's sleeve and injected him.

"Isn't he a good doggie?" Val said. "Good little doggie."

Roy had slipped away. Dora followed him, not wanting to be left alone with Val, nor watching Trevor falling into the unwitting sleep they fell into with the doctor's help.

Roy strode across the yard with a long hook. She'd seen him carry this down to the coast and back up before. He walked to the caravan and seemed to tilt almost backwards, as if praying to both heaven and hell at the same time, heaven with his eyes, hell with the back of his head.

She saw nothing, but he seemed to. He shuddered, stretched up, lifted his hook and swung it quickly. He caught something, because he tugged and pulled, walking backwards as if dragging a large animal.

"Got him," he said to Dora, his eyes gleaming, his teeth yellow and sharp.

He'd caught a ghost with his hook. She'd not been so close to them before, but this one was almost discernible as a person. She could see features: a large nose, long hair. Long arms that seemed to stretch and stretch, but he was holding on to a tree stump, trying to stop himself from being dragged.

With a proficient flick, Roy lifted him and moved forward, into the house, along the dark hallway, towards Dora's room.

The ghost grew less resistant as they moved along. In fact he seemed to crawl quickly, helping the forward motion, and by the time they reached Dora's room, he leapt forward, landing face down on Trevor.

Val screamed, but then it was quiet; she was so terrified now, so stunned, that her voice box froze.

"Dora's doorway," Roy said. "This is a good room. The ghosts are here. If you can shift the way you see, you'll see them. The hook is a trick. Like I was saying. You can con a ghost as easily as you can con a person."

Trevor began to mumble. The doctor had left and Val sat in the room, bending forward.

"See? Even talks when he's going to sleep," she said.

Dora wasn't sure why she was allowed to stay, but she had mastered the art of invisibility. She'd long ago learned that unless she spoke, she'd often be ignored.

"Here are my words," Trevor said, but it wasn't him. The voice was deeper, more confident.

She paced the hallway. In the breakfast room the clock ticked and she saw that it was three minutes to noon. She paused, absorbing the silence that seemed to always come. She thought she could hear two voices coming from her room, two young voices.

Her daughters. Her daughters calling.

She raced down the corridor, but there were no young voices at all, just the dead husband, moaning on about an unfair life.

Trevor was older than her, but handsome and filled with life. She looked at the old woman, Val, and thought she saw drool on the woman's chin.

"She's not long for here, stupid bitch. She'll be rotted from the outside in and deserve every painful second of it."

Seemed even more awful to hear these words from kind Trevor's mouth. More and more spewed out, hurtful words that made sense to Val but not to the rest of them; before long she was curled over in her chair, her hands over her ears.

"You can wait outside, Val. We'll hear him out. I'll ask him for the combination," Roy said. Val nodded and stumbled from the room.

You can con a ghost as easily as you can con a live person, Roy had said. He said to Trevor, "Prove to me you're who you say you are. Tell me something only you know. Tell me a number. Tell me the combination to your safe. I'll keep it to myself."

"My wife is an idiot with numbers."

"I hate numbers," Val whispered to Dora in the hall. Her voice quavered more than it should in a woman her age.

Trevor gave the combination over and spoke some more and then mumbled himself into silence.

Dora found Val standing on the front veranda.

"Garden could do with some work." Val said, as if nothing had happened. "I've been having a nice chat with this gentleman."

Mr. Cox hummed and smiled. He spent most of his time swinging in the swing chair, reading and napping. He could only sleep when there was movement. He said he hoped to die in his sleep. He said that powerful stuff happened if you died in your sleep. If you died while subconscious was in the forefront.

Roy had written down the number. "Do you want to wait for Trevor to wake up?" he said, and Val shrugged.

"I'm not even sure I'm awake. Or dreaming. What is this, anyway? Pretty sure I'm asleep. Down on the beach. On the sand. It's so warm I'm going to get burned, aren't I? Skin cancer. And every one of you will say I told you so."

"We won't say I told you so," Dora said. "Because we couldn't give a shit."

"Let's get this safe open. Let's see if it works," Roy said. His voice was uneven, as if he was terrified of what they were about to confirm.

Val wouldn't go with them. Only Roy and Dora, two observers.

"I feel as if we should be recording this or something," Roy said. "Because no one will believe us."

"It's not going to work," Dora said.

But it did. He dialed the numbers Trevor had spoken, and the safe opened.

"Jesus fucken Christ," Roy said. "It fucken worked."

"You've had proof before, Roy. The message on the beach that told you where the deeds were, and there were others."

"Yeah, that was bullshit. I found the deeds under one of the mattresses. This is real."

Inside were a few piles of money, two small boxes filled with jewelry that looked like gold, and some photos. The first one showed Val's first husband, naked and proud, his hand protectively resting on the head of a young man. Dora didn't want to look at the rest of the photos.

They would burn them, not show them to Val. She didn't need to see them; Roy and Dora agreed this without saying.

Roy pocketed one of the jewelry boxes ("These bastards won't pay me, you watch.") and they went out to give the rest to Val.

He handed her the items and she stared at them, disbelieving. She sat on the front veranda, unmoving, until Trevor woke up and came to join her. Then Roy showed them to their room.

~

Dora curled up in the big armchair in the lounge room. The painter was there, humming to himself, creating, and she loved spending this quiet time there. This empty, thoughtless time, this interim, this hiatus, before she had to face what she now knew.

If there was an afterlife, she would have to atone.

If there was an afterlife, her girls could still hate her. Or perhaps they loved her. Forgave her. Understood her.

If she could bring them here, she'd know

She could confess. Tell them she was sorry. And, surely, they would then forgive her, and they would be able to rest.

She'd planned to stop it. She had. But she wanted to hear from her girls.

SIXTH DAY
SUNDAY
AFTERNOON/NIGHT

She watched the painter flick his hair out of his eyes over and over again. Then she said, "Would you like a haircut? I'm good at it. I can just do the floppy bit in the front if you like or give you a full on makeover."

He laughed. "Moi? I haven't had a haircut in years."

"Oh, really?" she said, smiling at him. She wanted to cut hair. She wanted to cut his. This was a good thing, because cutting hair centered her, and she hadn't touched a strand for months.

"I'll grab my kit. Meet you in the back courtyard."

They called it a courtyard, but really it was just a small tiled area with a few old chairs stacked in it.

She went to her car for her haircutting kit. She never traveled without it; kept it there rather than inside and she'd never been sure why. It's not like she'd had a dangerous life that she'd need to escape from in a hurry, just a dull and very mean one.

Dora set the painter up and got to work. Others watched through their windows and then came down to join them bringing drinks and crap food. She did what she could for him; cleaned him up. Transformed how he appeared. But he still had the same facial tics. The same nervous gestures. Still. He looked younger, almost handsome.

She proceeded to Roy's hair, cutting it into a modern style. He had good hair, quite thick and surprisingly healthy. She'd made him shower before she touched him and even given him her soap, so he smelled familiar and clean.

"Go put some good clothes on before I blow dry it. Then we'll get the full effect."

He stared at her. She hadn't let him look at himself yet.

"Your funeral clothes," Val said. She and Trevor were watching it all, Trevor with a dazed, empty look about him. "Or you could borrow one of Trevor's suits. Lord knows that man has a lot of clothes."

In one of Trevor's suits, with his hair done, Roy looked good.

"Close your mouth Roy," Dora said, and they actually gasped at how handsome he looked.

"Me next!" the doctor said.

Dora ran her fingers through his hair. "You do need a touch up. Someone needs to go to the supermarket to pick up some hair dye."

"I'll go," Val said. "At least I'll get the right one." She wore the jewelry they'd found in the safe and seemed softer. Dora wasn't sure they'd done the right thing in not showing her the photos, but she thought they had.

They all queued up, wanting a cut, and she said, "Pay me in food," to Mrs. Reddy and "Pay me in kind," to Luke.

For a moment, standing in the late afternoon sunshine, all of them neat and clean, transformed, they could have been anywhere. Dora felt almost at peace. Almost good.

"You're smiling," Luke said. "Good to see. We've all chosen the compromise here. We're all thinking life will improve. We're clinging on to the last hope, keeping a roof over our heads, as crappy and leaky as the roof might be."

Val returned with bags of shopping: dye for everyone, snacks, drinks. Expensive treats none of them could afford. Dora saw tears in her eyes as the group descended and felt an affinity for her in that moment. It was nice to help. To be useful.

The doctor was next. His hair was an awful red and Dora told him she'd dye it a good dark brown. "It's not common for a man to dye his hair," she said. "Especially an older man. You have to be subtle about it."

"I've always done it," he said. "For years, anyway. I had a step-daughter who wanted to dye her hair purple. Her mum wouldn't let her, but she asked me. I said no, though. I never did help her dye her hair. Never did."

"You didn't?"

"No! They said I got agitated and killed her. I didn't. I really didn't."

There was silence. This was past; they didn't talk about the past.

Val said, "God, it's stuffy in the rooms. The windows don't open. It stinks in there."

"That's what I try to tell them," Roy said, "when they stop me trying to make the rooms smell nice. Every occupant leaves a trace. Deliberate or accidental. Some you'd think would leave nothing at all. Not the vaguest of memories. But they all leave a stink of themselves."

Freesia had joined them by now, and she collected all the hair. "You can't let a witch get it," she said. "That's bad luck."

"You honestly think we can have shittier lives than this?" the painter said.

Dora kept cutting. She didn't want to think about that. While she cut hair she didn't think about the words coming out of Trevor's mouth, the number he spoke. Or about her children and all that she'd lost. Freesia collected all the hair up and burned it, filling the small courtyard with a nasty stink.

Freesia put her arm through Luke's possessively, but he barely acknowledged her existence. He looked tired, wiped out, as if he'd been running for hours. His defenses were down and he looked haunted and Dora thought: *It's not what he's seen, it's what he's done. Never married, but always falling in love—always desperately, let's-elope-in-love. With the girl in the supermarket who asked him to help her reach a jar on the top shelf, or was it the older lady who seemed nice and lively and smelled of cake and icing? The things he's done; he's beaten women, he's got that violence in him. He's only relaxed when he sleeps and he can hardly sleep.*

His haircut was still very military. Very close to the head. She thought it made him feel like a member of the club. It was growing out a bit, though, so she said, "Trim?" and he gratefully sat for it.

She liked the feel of his head. It was firm, with a few bumps and dents. She liked the feel of his shoulders against her breasts, and she leaned forward into him, and he leaned back, and it was very, very sexy.

"Let me cut yours, Dora," Freesia said. "I have a beauty diploma."

"Same as Julia!" Dora said.

"Your hair looks like a mop!" Freesia said. "When was the last time you had it cut?"

Freesia had lied about having a diploma. She sheared one side of Dora's hair down to stubble and laughed about it. Dora didn't realize what she was doing until it was done, because it seemed impossible.

"You're a fucking bitch, Freesia," Luke said. "And she still looks a shitload better than you ever will."

This ended the session.

Dora headed to her room, but only made it as far as Roy's office. He caught her, calling out, "Don't forget you're doing Sunday dinner. You have to cook before you can eat, so unless you never want dinner, you have to cook."

She had been warned about this but had forgotten.

"I don't have any money for ingredients," she said. "And I just cut everyone's hair."

"I'll show you where everything is," he said, ignoring her. He led her to the kitchen behind the breakfast room.

"Mr. Cox will pay, won't you, Mr. Cox?" He was already sitting waiting in the breakfast room. Mr. Cox looked haunted, as if he was hearing voices. He'd slept with the ghosts so many times, ghost voices leaked through. He was tiny, his feet dangling from the chair, barely touching. "Dinner won't be for hours, mate. But we need cash to get the stuff."

Mr. Cox pulled out his wallet and handed over $40. "Receipt and change," he said.

Dora was exhausted, but she understood about dutiful cooking, so she walked to the local supermarket and bought mince, lasagna sheets, tomato sauce, and onions to cook the lasagna recipe she'd found on the internet. It felt so strange to be out in the real world. Even stranger than it had a week ago. She felt even less a part of it. She bought napkins with sea shells on them and it gave her a ridiculous amount of pleasure imagining what the others would think.

Julia came to help cook, or watch and keep company, at least. She could barely stand. "That last one was very hard," she said.

"Yeah," the doctor said. He, too, was in the kitchen. "Yeah, that ghost said, 'Can I go, now? I've said my piece. I've got no more words left.' But if he had no more words he'd be gone. That's what's happened to the others. And true enough, poor Julia jerked and started again."

He mimicked her, jerking and shaking his arms.

Julia looked pale and drawn, as if part of her had been sucked away. "We really shouldn't let Roy do this."

The doctor said, "No one is being hurt."

But there was damage. You could see it. People less energetic. Losing some of their will, and most of them had little to begin with. Dora could see it even if they didn't.

Julia said she loved the sleep it brought her. The peace. "There are no dreams in that sleep. You can't get caught by surprise."

Dora found this true, too. She wasn't rested, but her mind had been still.

Julia said, "You need to be unconscious for it to work. My brother spoke in his coma sometimes. It didn't sound like him. Roy says if my brother comes through he'll let me hear it. He will come, one day. He's making his way to me now. Coming for this." She held up a tobacco tin. "Used to keep his wacky tobaccy in here."

⁓

The lasagna came out okay. She put it out to serve, but only Mr. Cox was there. He began eating noisily. The others would arrive later, in dribs and drabs.

"How is it?" she asked him. He had whisky that he shared with her.

"Tasty," he said. "What's the secret recipe?"

"Can't share a secret!" she said.

"Some secrets are big, some secrets are small. I don't know what I did anymore. What they did. Who took the children."

"I was thinking I could talk to my children. I know them. I'll understand what they're saying. Do you think?"

"You can try. But be ready to hear the worst. And I'm not the one for it. Too many voices in this head."

⁓

The indent of Trevor's head on her pillow. The smell of Val's perfume.

It was late and she was exhausted. She lay in the dent Trevor had made on her mattress and closed her eyes. But soon, so soon, a ghost began to fill her room like a marshmallow expanding in the microwave. He was a big man, morbidly obese, walking over and back over her bed with great purpose. She was shaken to the core, freezing cold. She thought, *is this Val's dead husband*? But he was slight, thin, not enormous like this.

She'd seen him naked in the photo; she knew what he looked like.

Dora slid out of bed and backed out of her room. She was sure she could smell him, feel him. He turned his head as she slid the door open, and his face creased with a look of fury.

She couldn't run; she felt frozen. She backed up the hallway, watching for him to come after her, not wanting him to notice her.

She backed into Roy, hovering outside his office.

She pointed at her room. "He's . . ."

"Ah, you've met the old inhabitant," Roy said. "He died in your room. They had to knock the wall down to get him out. That's why you've got a new door. Listen," he said. "Listen, I want you do to something for me."

He beckoned her into his office. Draped over the desk was an antique dress made of a dark, shiny cloth. Not silk. It looked like shiny, thick cotton, with embroidery almost covering it.

"I want you to wear it." He was an old man and she'd never seen anything like interest in sex from him. "I'll give you a month's free board to wear it to bed," he said. "You don't want to be awake when they come through you. You hear a ghost talk from inside your own head, you'll never be the same."

"It is beautiful," she said. It really was. She could see it was damaged by water in places, and there were rents that had been poorly mended.

"I call myself the receiver of the wreck," Roy said. "Not official. But who is, these days? Used to be. Used to be. For me it's receiving the people as well as the things, and who else can say they are willing to do that?"

He held the dress out.

"I want you to wear this dress. It came from the wreck and I think it was the captain's wife's dress. Or his girlfriend. Or he made the cabin boy wear it so he probably came all over it. Right? Like any man has done. Any girl has a dress like this.

"The captain is a big one. From all the things all the others have said we've pieced together his story."

"You could just lay it over me while I'm asleep. Nice of you to ask, I guess."

"It always works best if the person knows. Is willing. It can get ugly otherwise."

"I'll do it, but you need to do something in return. I want to go to the place my daughters . . . and see if we can bring back their ghosts. See if we can talk to them."

Roy said, "Wear the dress. We'll give you a good night's sleep. And in return, we'll see if we can drag your girls back home."

She made him leave the room while she pulled the dress on. It seemed to settle on her like a curse; she could feel it clinging to her, seeping into her bones like oil.

"What if I get marshmallow man? He seems angry."

"Most of them are. But I'm like a matchmaker. I try to put people together who'll get along."

He wasn't very good at it, Dora thought. Then the doctor came, and Dora slept.

SEVENTH DAY
TUESDAY
BREAKFAST

Dora woke up hungry. This never happened, not since she was a kid, training for the hundred-meter race, going to bed early after hours at the pool.

She was hungry. She sat up quickly, keen to get to breakfast, but felt dizzy so sat still for a moment.

Her pajamas were limp with sweat. She stood to go to the bathroom, her stomach rumbling. It felt like her bladder was about to burst.

The sign said *vacant*. It usually did. On her floor there were two construction workers, men she hadn't met, and they kept different hours. The shower was filthy today, the floor covered with grime. It made her dry retch to look at it.

The wee almost hurt and she hoped she didn't have a yeast infection. Washing her hands, she glanced up in the mirror. She never liked looking at herself but you couldn't help it here.

There was already a dark shadow on the side of her head. Her hair was growing back very quickly.

Her throat hurt.

It was baked beans and toast for breakfast. But it should have been spaghetti if it was Monday. *It must be Tuesday*, she thought.

"How'd you sleep?" Roy asked.

"Did he come?" she asked Roy. He shook his head. "You got someone else. It was good, all you got, but not the captain. You'll try again. Won't you?"

She didn't answer. She said, "You still have to take me to my girls," and he nodded.

"We're going to see if we can get my girls today," she told the room, and the rest of them clamored in, all saying *get my loved one.* The doctor wanted his sister. Julia wanted her brother. All of them clamoring at Roy, saying *fuck you, I deserve this too.*

"None of the rest of you were smart enough to think of it, were you?" Roy said.

~

"Do you have something of theirs? Something to call them with?"

She showed him the hairbrushes, identical except one had a sticker of a unicorn, one a sticker of a panda.

She held the brushes close to her heart as they walked to her car.

Dora had not driven her car since she arrived at the rooming house. It felt strange but also familiar to be behind the wheel. Not in any way comforting. The youngest one's safety seat was still in place, and there were story tapes all over the floor. One in the player; she'd never take that out.

"It's not too far?" Roy said. "I can't go too far."

It was four suburbs over, and he was okay with that.

The familiarity of all of it made her feel ill. She pulled into her driveway (one bump, a crack in the concrete) and stopped. "This is my place."

"This is a shithole. I never pictured you living in a shithole."

"Yeah, well. You marry a loser, you live in a shithole. The backyard is nice, though."

"They died here?"

She'd turned the car off. "No . . . it was instinct, coming back."

She took him to the place, the Safe House. The sign had been taken down, thank god, but there was nothing else to indicate what had happened.

"Yeah," Roy said. "Now I feel it. It's a fucken curse I have, I swear."

They walked around the side of the house. It seemed empty but you could never be sure.

"Yeah," he said. "There's someone here,"

"Who is it?"

"Just one. Only one. Here."

He lifted his hook and spun slowly, then edged forward like a dogcatcher after a stray dog. He shook, and sweat dripped off him although the day was cold.

"Someone," he said. "Someone else who died here."

She hadn't said. Not even to herself, because that death was on her, too.

"My husband . . . when he found out. He came here. Before the police did. They found the man dead. You never know who's capable of murder."

Roy lifted his hook. "He's coming with us whether you want him to or not. He's got things to say. He must have used the brushes."

"They always had them," Dora said. "They'd take brushes and forget their lunches. Easily tangled hair. Like mine. They liked to brush."

"He used the brushes." With speed, he hooked at something in the air and began to drag. She could see the ghost forming; a man, quite short, very muscly.

"No, not him! Not him! The girls. My girls."

"They're not here. Be happy about that. Not here. Gone elsewhere."

She watched him with disbelief. He turned to go back to the car and then stopped. She watched his whole body shiver.

"Come on," he said.

SEVENTH DAY
TUESDAY
NIGHT

Roy had to drive back. Dora couldn't. She was struck dumb, struck blind, struck numb. She'd thought she'd speak to her girls. She wanted to hear, "Mummy, we love you. Mummy, not your fault," but he said they were gone. She knew she should be happy, her girls released like that, but all she wanted to do was sleep. She couldn't see the dead man, but she felt him and knew he was with them, sitting on her lap, perhaps, because she felt a pressure there and she could smell him, a stink of fried onions and burned cheese. As Roy pulled in front of the house (and he was a terrible driver, complaining all the way that he had to do it, almost killing them twice in collisions) she threw herself out of the car and ran inside, into her room, and took two sleeping pills, wanting to numb it. Stop it. But stupid. Stupid. Why would she sleep, and she didn't even think of this until they were down her gullet, why would she sleep when he was on his way?

She couldn't sleep.

She curled up in bed, forcing her eyes closed because otherwise they dried up in her head. A day or two; she didn't know. Walking overheard as if someone was wearing army boots or they were going bowling. Walking over her, she felt feet, felt the pressure of feet on her bed, and smells of them seeped in to her dreams.

~

A knock on the door. Roy. "Trevor is going to have a sleep. If you want to listen you can, or I can tell you what he says."

She wasn't sure she could bear it but wanted to hear it firsthand.

She didn't want it watered down; she wanted to know what the man who'd killed her daughters said. What were their last words? She'd ask him that. Did they love her?

She'd ask him that, too. Trevor waited in his room, one of the nicer ones that cost a bit more. The walls were painted a pale yellow and the ceiling was much higher than in other rooms. There was a cupboard, too, set in the wall, and windows to let the light in. He had a shelf of Roy's books and a collection of romance novels.

Val wasn't there, and Dora didn't ask where she was. She kissed Trevor's hand. "I hope this doesn't hurt too much. I don't think he's a nice man."

"I'm a nice man," Trevor said, kissing her hand back. "He can't beat me."

He lay down on his bed. Roy placed the hairbrushes beside him. He didn't say anything for a while, although he started to shake. The doctor watched him, mouthed *he's okay*.

Then Trevor started to stroke his own hair. Stroke, stroke, stroke. "Such pretty hair," he said, his voice soft, like a whisper. "Such lovely brushes. I wish I had long hair like them."

Trevor brushed his own hair. Dora felt her fists clench. She wanted to pummel him, punch his face until his nose bled.

"Run run fast as you can," he said, and "the bones the bones the bones bury the bones."

Dora said, "Did they say they loved me?" and Trevor startled, half-sat up.

"Did they? Did they say I was good to them?"

"These little ones have no mum. These little ones are running because they are hungry. I made them cheese on toast but they didn't eat it."

Trevor started to mumble.

"I gave them McDonalds," Dora said. She didn't know who she was telling. "They weren't hungry. They should have come home to me.'

"The bones the bones bury the bones," he said, then he clutched his chest. Trevor's eyes opened wide and dark. Dora jumped forward, wanting to see into them, see what was reflected, but nothing.

The doctor moved her aside. "Fuck, I think he's having a seizure. Old bastard. You shouldn't have got him to do this. Fuck fuck fuck." The doctor loosened Trevor's collar. "Get out, give me room, call an ambulance," he said, and they did all of those things.

~

Most of the residents watched the ambulance drive away. "Did you hear your daughters?" they asked her and she shook her head, "but almost," she said, "and he spoke about them," so they were all at Roy, *get my sister, get my brother,* and he said, "It's not manageable. I can't control it. We don't want these people in the house." He said as an aside to Dora, "He said to bury the bones. I think we should bury the bones and see if that calls the captain. You promised you'd try again."

She didn't ask what bones; bones filled the place. She'd seen them in alcoves, hanging on walls, propping up books.

"What good do you think that will do?"

"It's an old wrecker's superstition. Whoever finds the body has to bury it." Roy said. "I bet there were plenty who didn't do it."

They walked around the rooming house. There were more bones than Dora had noticed before, some over doors, some hiding behind books.

She felt she was moving step by step, surviving minute by minute. She felt bad that Trevor had been so powerfully affected, but angry, also, that he had told her nothing. She thought he deserved the pain, that he should have dug harder, he should have attached himself to that murderer and told her more.

There was no grass in the tiny tiled back courtyard so they went out the front garden. They were joined there by Luke, Freesia, Larry, and Mr. Cox. Roy laid down a bone he'd chosen, one long and human, on a plastic mat and formed minced meat around it. Then he wrapped it in plastic wrap.

"The body's long gone so we'll make him a new one. He deserves the best," Roy said, although Dora could see it wasn't the best mince, but hamburger mince run through with fat and gristle.

They covered more bones this way.

Roy dug a hole, placed the meaty bones in and covered them up. "They're all the bones I have," he said.

~

She wondered about the killer's message, to bury the bones. She wondered what else the killer had buried in the backyard.

She made an anonymous call to the police, telling them to dig hard, dig further.

~

Bones were found.

~

She felt strong enough to call her ex-husband in jail, to tell him, "You did the right thing. You saved other children by killing him."

He cried when she told him. She called him a hero, a good man.

~

She awakened to find Roy standing over her.

"Can you hear the clock? He's here. He's definitely here." He held the dress up for her again. "We need to give it a go. I'm just waiting for the doctor to come back."

"How's Trevor?"

He screwed up his face as if annoyed at her for being distracted.

"Luke can do it. He was the emergency medic onboard his ship," Dora said.

Luke had been quiet for days. He'd channeled a young boy and made the mistake of listening to his own voice after on a recording. He'd not wanted to see anyone. She'd dropped food off to him, taking plates of breakfast.

She went up to see him and asked him for a favor. "And watch over me," she said. "I don't want Roy groping me while I'm lying there and not moving."

~

"Where's my next puppet, ay? Who's the one keeps waking my men up, keeps waking my women up. Won't let us sleep. Curse on you. Curse on you and may your blood turn to rust, may you shrivel and live long in agony for what you've done.

    May your children be fatherless and your wife a widow.
    May your children be wandering beggars;
    may they be driven from their ruined homes.
    May a creditor seize all you have;
    may strangers plunder the fruits of your labor.
    May no one extend kindness to you
    or take pity on your fatherless children.
    May your descendants be cut off,
    their names blotted out from the next generation."

Dora spoke on and on and on until Roy cried out, leaped forward to try to smother her with a pillow, and Luke stepped up and elbowed him in the nose, which poured forth so much blood over her face she blinked her eyes open, sat up.

Then she really did fall into an exhausted sleep.

EIGHTH DAY
WEDNESDAY
BREAKFAST

There was no breakfast ready, so the tenants went into the kitchen and made do. There was bacon, spaghetti, eggs, baked beans; they cooked the lot, laughing as they did, feeling like rule-breakers.

Roy was gone and no one knew where. No one was bothered. Dora was the only one who knew why; her carefully designed words, her fake captain, had made him run.

Dora felt lighter, as if the place had emptied out of the mess.

"Check us out," Julia said. "We're survivors. We really are. We are still here. Forget about how hard it is, how failed we seem; we are still alive, when many others aren't. We are survivors."

The day was cold and wet. They all dragged blankets onto the veranda and sat there, protected, watching birds bathe in the puddles, a stray dog hunch past.

"We're the lucky ones," Julia said.

And yet even as they sat there, enjoying their coffee, Luke came through the door.

"They're still coming," he said, and he seemed so frail Dora had him sit down before he fell. The clock ticked and the sound of the sea seemed louder, too, and they all went to stand on the road to watch the ghosts drag themselves up the hill.

Dora felt a terrible tiredness, a weariness so deep she had to lie down. The others, too, all of them so tired they couldn't make it to their bedrooms but curled up there on the veranda, and closed their eyes, and waited for the ghosts to come.

~

Psalm 109 (the "cursing psalm"): *And he donned a curse like his garment, and it came into his midst like water and into his bones like oil.*

THE END

About the Author

Kaaron Warren published her first short story in 1993 and has had stories in print every year since. Her stories have appeared in Australia, the US, China, the UK, and elsewhere in Europe, and have been selected for both Ellen Datlow's and Paula Guran's Best of the Year Anthologies.

Kaaron has lived in Melbourne, Sydney, Canberra and Fiji. She has published five novels (*Slights, Walking the Tree, Mistification, The Grief Hole* and *Tide of Stone*) and seven short story collections, including the multi-award winning *Through Splintered Walls*. Her most recent short story collection is *A Primer to Kaaron Warren* from Dark Moon Books.

Her novella "Sky" from that collection won the Shirley Jackson Award and was shortlisted for the World Fantasy Award. It went on to win all three of the Australian genre awards, as did *The Grief Hole* in 2017. In 2019, *Tide of Stone* won an Aurealis Award and a Shadows award and was shortlisted for the Locus award, and her novella *Crisis Apparition* from *A Primer to Kaaron Warren* won an Aurealis award.

Kaaron was a Fellow at the Museum for Australian Democracy, where she researched prime ministers, artists and serial killers. In 2018 she was the Established Artist in Residence at Katharine Susannah Prichard House in Western Australia. She's taught workshops in haunted asylums, old morgues and second hand clothing shops and she's mentored several writers through a number of programs.

She was Guest of Honor at the World Fantasy Convention in 2018, New Zealand's Geysercon in 2019, and Stokercon 2019.